# SC

# DEATH

Half way up the stairs she almost choked with fright. *What if he is?* she thought. *What if he killed them? And he's walking right behind – And I've got my nightdress on, which is no protection at all. What if he really did? What if he slips a knife between my shoulder blades? Oh God, oh God. What am I doing here? How did I ever get into such a mess as this?*

He was walking right behind; she could feel him touching her dress—

*Oh help me, God*, she thought.

*Other titles in the Point Crime series:*

*Shoot the Teacher*
by David Belbin

*Look out for:*

*Overkill*
by Alane Ferguson

*The Smoking Gun*
by Malcolm Rose

*Baa Baa Dead Sheep*
by Jill Bennett

*Avenging Angel*
by David Belbin

# POINT CRIME

# SCHOOL FOR DEATH

## Peter Beere

SCHOLASTIC

Scholastic Children's Books,
Scholastic Publications Ltd,
7–9 Pratt Street, London NW1 0AE

Scholastic Inc.,
730 Broadway, New York, NY 10003, USA

Scholastic Canada Ltd,
123 Newkirk Road, Richmond Hill,
Ontario, Canada L4C 3G5

Ashton Scholastic Pty Ltd,
P O Box 579, Gosford, New South Wales,
Australia

Ashton Scholastic Ltd,
Private Bag 1, Penrose, Auckland,
New Zealand

First published by Scholastic Publications Ltd, 1993

Copyright © 1993 by Peter Beere

ISBN 0 590 55191 4

Typeset by Quadraset Ltd, Midsomer Norton, Avon
Printed by Cox & Wyman Ltd, Reading, Berks

# Prologue

It was the autumn term, the start of a new year. A time to begin again and wipe the old slate clean. A time to make new friends, renew ones from the past. A time for – *Drowning*.

Alison was drowning in darkness, black water closing around her, thick water in her throat and choking up her lungs, cold fingers stroking her. Cold waters lapped in her nostrils; her stomach cramped, her legs stirred up clinging mud; her hands grasped leaves and stems which folded in her grasp, her arms beat lilies down. Alison was drowning in the pond at Summervale, a place of excellence, a school for well-bred girls. Alison was drifting down through a silvered, moonlit pool – like a Gothic heroine.

But wait – a figure moved across the bare black rock which was the cliff of Summervale's unlit west wing: a frail and ghost-like form, blonde-haired, a snow-white gown; fleet figure racing down. A figure sliding down the lurching bank which dropped down from the field towards the reed-fringed lake. Down through the ferns and docks and tangled beds of thorn, through moonlit tracts and shade.

A voice cried – "*Alison!*"

A desperate, sudden lunge – a veil of hissing spray sent through the star-touched night. "*I'm going – can't breathe, can't see—*"

"I'm coming, Alison! Try to hold on!" cried Kate.

Kate Stone was screaming, trying to alert the school, trying to call out some help, bring men with boats and poles – but there was nothing there; no hands to split the gloom; no help to match her own.

As if on slippery, sliding boards she crept upon her knees along a landing stage to which two punts were moored. Two ancient rotted punts which needed more than prayers to bring them back again.

The old stage was rocking as water lapped its piles. Dark bugs crawled through the ooze which spilled between its boards. Kate's hand went reaching out – Ali thrashed, sank again: Kate screamed out "*Alison!*"

Then total darkness. No sound, no gleam of light. A heavy, rolling cloud obscured the hunter's moon. There was no glint of stars reflected in the lake – just silent sluggish slime. There was a swirl of bubbles: an empty, hollow sound. The vast expanse of black heaved up like lazy tar. A monster of the night which had devoured its prey now settled down to snooze. Kate thrashed the water; her arms plunged in its depths, reaching for Ali's hand, her face, her sleeve, her hair; trying to drag Ali back, her chum, her friend for life – Ali the bloated corpse.

*"Oh, Ali – Alison!"*

You can't bring back the dead. But Ali jerked awake, and said, "What's going on?"

"You had another dream. You've got to cut them out, you're going to wake the school."

"Another dream?" Ali sat up in the bed, the sheet wrapped round her legs where she had thrashed and fought. "I had another dream?"

Kate nodded. "Always dreams. Can't you sleep peacefully?"

There in the darkness – the gleam from Ali's clock; the pale of thin night-clothes, Kate's falling golden curls. The snoring from the gloom where Maxine dreamed the dreams Ali would like to dream.

Ali said – "I remember. I was drowning in the

lake. You came down through the thorns to try to rescue me."

Kate's cool hand touched her arm. "Just try to go to sleep. It was a nightmare."

Alison shivered as she looked around the room where four girls shared their lives, their hopes, their thoughts, their dreams. She said, "I dream too much. I must have inner fears – I dream of death and things. I keep remembering—" her hands moved to her face. Her eyes looked big and wide inside her thin pale face. "I think of all the deaths – the water in my eyes – that's the worst way to die."

Kate's cold hands shook her. "I think they're all bad ways." But she was smiling now as Ali settled down. "Will you go back to sleep? No one is going to drown. No one is going to die."

"No," Ali whispered as she shuffled down the bed, and pulled the covers tight to keep bad dreams away.

"Try to have pleasant dreams."

"I don't want any at all."

"Good night, Ali."

There in the darkness. The night sounds of the school. The sense of crushing weight from its thick granite walls. The long draught-haunted rooms; the gloom and creaking floors. Dark halls of Summervale. But it *was* Summervale – a place of friends and trust. A place where fear is rare and only comes in dreams. A place where girls grow wise, have plans of hope and joy. Ali lay back and dreamed. . . .

# 1

**8**.20 Monday, and the breakfast bell had sounded, and the clattering of several dozen feet rang through the corridors. In one corner of the sixth-form shower block, by the last of a row of ceramic grey-white sinks, Kate and Alison were trying furiously to appear presentable.

"My skin looks hideous," said Kate. "It's turning grey. I miss my beauty sleep through all these dreams of yours." She tugged her long blonde hair and rubbed her pale blue eyes. "My body's changing shape."

Alison laughed. She, like Kate, was blonde and slim, but not as tall as Kate, nor was she quite as old. Ali was just sixteen, while Kate was pushing on towards her next birthday.

She spat out toothpaste. "You're like a beauty queen."

"I'm not, I'm hideous. I'm like Susie Minter now. No one will fancy me and it's all your fault. I think you're ruining me." Kate straightened gracefully, until she was ramrod straight, the effect of an upbringing by army parents. They were somewhere overseas, though she was never quite sure where. "My boobs are hollowing."

The two girls turned around as, by strange coincidence, poor Susie Minter happened to look in the room. But the two friends scowled at her and sent her scuttling off. She was a total bore.

"She's got three nipples," said Kate through veils of hair.

"Who? Susie Minter has?"

"Yes, that's what Maxine said. She saw them in the shower."

"You can't have three nipples."

"Some people have more than that." Kate smoothed her eyebrows out. "Dogs have got ten nipples."

"She's not a dog, though."

"She's pretty close to it." Kate tried to flatten out her skirt, but its once-neat navy pleats resisted all attempts. She smoothed her cotton blouse – thin stripes of grey on white. "I'll get told off for this. Looks like I slept in it."

"*Which is what Mrs Locke will say!*"

"*You girl! Did you sleep in that?*" they cried in unison.

"No, 'cause it wasn't my turn – somebody else had it!" Kate gave a joyous shriek. "What a fat old bag she is."

"But very neatly ironed."

"*You girl! Don't run, don't cough!*"

"*Don't fold your legs like that. You'll end up like a tart—*"

"*You're like a Jezebel!*" The two girls jostled arms. "Come on, or we're going to be late." Kate put her things away. They hurried down the hall towards the breakfast room.

"Is this skirt straight at the back?"

"Yes, it's your legs that are bent."

"How *très charmant* you are." Kate performed a graceful swirl as she swept into the room, late for the toast again. . . .

"Good morning, girls."

The girls were all on their feet. "Good morning, Mrs Day."

Mrs Day smiled at them. She was dressed all in grey: grey skin, grey hair, grey clothes, like someone's grandmother. She set her glasses straight. "And are we having fun?"

"Oh yes, Mrs Day," they said.

She nodded absently. "That's very good," she said, and waved a thin grey hand, which meant they could sit down. She peered around her desk as if it might have changed. "Today is my birthday. But that's irrelevant." The old lady gave a sigh. "I'm sixty-two today. What other day is this? Monday – of course it is. And Mr Bleak's been out collecting scrummy things, since we debated – what?"

"Environments and things," said Lynsey Dickerson from the back.

"*Environments and things.*" Mrs Day sighed again. "We call them habitats, but we will let that pass. Today is Choice Chambers. We have some little pets."

The girls looked round as the classroom door swung back, and Mr Bleak limped in with a deep plastic tub. He was a thin brown man, dressed in a thin brown coat. His job was to tend the labs.

"Mr Bleak's been busy. Did you get them, Mr Bleak?"

"I got you eighty-four," he said, as he put the tub on the desk. He tugged his brown coat straight, and dusted off his palms. He didn't raise a smile.

"Good." Mrs Day smiled as Mr Bleak limped out, trailing a twisted leg which had nothing wrong with it. He did it to spook the girls. It was his idea of a joke. He could have run in marathons.

"We have some woodlice here—"

All eyes fell on the tub.

"And you have Choice Chambers – one dish between each group. We are going to see how woodlice act when they are given a choice. Now doesn't that sound like fun?"

*She was floating face downwards amongst the fringing reeds. She wore a yellow dress; her skin was pure and white. Her hair had spread itself like the rays of a setting sun. Her eyes were clear and bright.*

*But they could not see anything, for she was as cold as ice. The blood lay still in her veins, no breath passed through her throat. No thoughts ran through her mind, no heart beat in her chest.*

*She wore the look of death. . . .*

"Right, so what we are looking for," said Mrs Day cheerfully, "is the way that woodlice react when they are given a choice. They can stay inside the light, or move into the dark half of the petri dish. We have to time this – have you all got your clocks?"

Eighteen girls gave a grunt, and shoved their clocks around.

"I've put your work-sheets out with the instructions on. I think that's all you need. Now, one girl from each group can pick your woodlice out—"

There wasn't a frantic rush to come out to the front.

"There's eighty-four of them. You can pick ten out each."

Feet started shuffling.

"You go and pick them," said Ali gloomily.

Kate looked straight in her eyes. "I really hate those things."

"Just scrape them in the dish."

"*You* scrape them in the dish."

They turned towards Maxine, who shared the desk with them. Maxine was preening herself; she did a lot of that. "Don't look at me," she said. "I've just been doing my nails."

"You don't mind things like that," said Kate.

They heard a stifled scream from someone at the front.

Maxine eyed them dubiously. "I don't like bugs and things."

"But these aren't really bugs."

"What are they, butterflies?" Maxine let out a sigh, and sat and stared them out. "I'm not going to go," she said.

"What if we all go up?" said Ali hopefully.

They thought about that one, and thought it seemed okay.

"But don't put one on me, or I will really scream," said Maxine earnestly.

# 2

The lesson ended abruptly just after ten o'clock, with a surprise announcement. It came as a relief to Lynsey and Susie Minter, who were having some problems with their experiment. They seemed to have picked a bunch of lousy *Onisci*, which would not perform for them.

"They're not doing anything," said Lynsey dismally. She was a tall, dark-haired, slim girl with freckles on her chin. "I think this lot's dead – they're all just lying there."

"Well, you keep poking them."

"But they're not doing anything, they're just sitting there. That one is eating itself—" Lynsey poked it with her pen. "Look, we've got six of them just lying on their backs. I don't think that's right."

"They might be sunbathing."

"Maybe the light's too bright—" Lynsey's voice petered out as Mrs Robbe came in. The tense school secretary was moving like the wind. She streaked across the room.

"Now what does she want?"

The girls sat back to watch as Mrs Robbe sped up to Mrs Day's grey desk, with her fast-clicking heels like the steps of startled birds. She bent down like a stork to speak in Mrs Day's ear—

"She'll peck old Day to death."

Mrs Robbe muttered something, and Mrs Day looked up with a short, sudden jerk. "Will you put your pens down, girls?"

"She must have pecked her brain," said Lynsey quietly.

Mrs Day rose to her feet as Mrs Robbe ran out. "We have to finish now, and go down to the hall."

"What's this, a fire drill?"

"Could be a bomb alert," said Kate, in Lynsey's ear.

Mrs Day picked her bag up. It was a grey affair. "Stop what you're doing now, and head off to the hall. Just leave your things behind and – stop that, Emily, they don't like too much heat."

Emily put a lamp down and stopped frying the lice, and Mrs Day gave a frown as she moved towards the door. "You're a disgusting child," she whispered under her breath, as groups of girls filed past.

"Are we coming back again?" said Lynsey at the door.

"Who knows? The luck I have, you'll all be here to stay." Mrs Day gave a smile. "Now hurry and catch up. We haven't too much time."

The hall was crowded. It whispered like a breeze as all the girls sat down on chairs of ancient wood. Three hundred chairs eased back and creaked on polished boards. Three hundred floorboards sighed.

This place was Summervale, dipped in antiquity; where former heads peered down from paintings on the walls. Where great deeds were proclaimed on ornate panelled walls, in understated scrolls. Here stood the names and the ghosts of Summervale, those who had made it big or sunk without a trace.

One more had just been joined to those who went before. Small chains of history. . . .

The girls were restless, and tried to look around while prefects in the aisles made them look straight ahead. Look straight towards the stage, where tutors in hushed ranks awaited Mrs Locke. This time was momentous: the girls could sense the shock which had infected staff and made them look so serious. They were not whispering. Something unique and stern had entered Summervale.

Ali nudged Lynsey, who was in the row ahead. "What do you think is going on?"

Lynsey did not look round. "I don't know. Could be drugs. The entire school is here. Even the domestics have been called out."

Ali glanced around and saw the kitchen staff, in a small, huddled group towards the rear of the hall. They all looked ill at ease, not used to being required to share in Summervale's news. Even Mr Bleak was there in his ill-fitting coat, his hands clamped to his sides as if out on parade. He still looked glum and sour, as if his life was cursed by the burden of his name. Mrs Day was sneezing at one side of the stage, beneath the thick red curtains Noah might have known. They hung in graceful curves, red velvet, gold brocade, fit to bedeck a king. Lights had been turned on to help the rain-swept day. They made the stage and staff look like a theatre set. They just required the star, the queen of this display. They needed Mrs Locke.

She came like diamonds, glittering in blue on black; the head of all the school, queen of all she surveyed. But she was strangely numb, distracted, not all there. She stared down at the ground. A man was with her, a tall, innocuous man, dressed in a long tan coat, unbuttoned to the waist. His hair was silver-grey, slicked down across his crown. His face was long and brown. The entire school stood up. The staff got to its feet. (Except for Mrs Fleck who had arthritic legs.) A silence deep as tombs descended on the hall. Mrs Locke's thick heels beat drums. She took her usual place behind the empty desk, which someone had sent back from the Crimean War. She put her papers down, and looked round for her chair. She told the school – "Sit down."

But Mrs Locke did not sit down herself. She stood beside her desk, then walked round to the front. The man in the long tan coat stood by like she was God, and he her courtier. She did not waste time. Her blue eyes embraced the school. She said, "I have some news which cannot be delayed. I am afraid that Miss Sagan, the school's new French mistress, has had an accident. She is no longer with us—"

"She must have left," breathed Kate.

"—She was found a short while ago, drowned in Four Acre Lake. I need not say how sad this news will make the whole school feel. This awful tragedy. . . ."

The hall was silent – it could barely take this in. Tutors did not die, they just turned old and grey. Tutors so full of fire, so bright and blessed with life – surely there's some mistake?

But there was no mistake. They only had to see the faces of the staff on stage to know how true this was. Claudine Sagan had drowned, not far from where they sat. The sixth-form girls were stunned. The young Headmistress appeared to age, simply standing on the stage; her hair seemed grey and flat, her skin found deeper lines. She seemed to lose the power of reverence she instilled, and shrink to normal size. She held one hand up to stem a rising tide of whispers which swelled up throughout the ancient hall. Grim prefects strode the aisles, long faces spitting fire on their ill-mannered hordes.

The murmurs petered out as the Headmistress looked around, and put her hand to her face as if at a loss for words. She said, "This kind of news will always be a shock, but we must be dignified." Mrs Locke took a deep breath. "In normal circumstances there would be little need for you to be involved, but in a case like this – of death by accident – other factors intervene. There is a police officer who would like to talk to you—" she glanced towards the man who stood beside her desk. "There are other police officers in the school, and if you know of anything that may be of some help, I trust you to pass it on.

"In the meantime normal lessons will be suspended, and we shall take a break until this afternoon. On *Friday* afternoon, inside the school chapel, we shall hold memorial prayers."

Mrs Locke left the stage in a total silence. All eyes were on the man dressed in the long tan coat. He took it off and sighed, and folded it over a chair. He said, "My name is Blair. . . ."

# 3

A bell was tolling as the girls stood in the rain
in the dark quadrangle which lay at the heart
of the school. They seemed reluctant to go inside,
knowing that death had stalked its gloomy halls.
The still, distant lake drew their eyes. In huddled
clusters they discussed the things they'd heard, trying to fill the gaps in the account of Miss Sagan's
death the previous night. Some called it suicide,
some said she must have died taking a moonlight
swim. But none of them knew her well, for she
hadn't been there long, though she had touched
them all with her unfettered charm. She had been
petite and dark, with deep brown, almond-shaped
eyes. She'd laughed like butterflies.

It was hard to recall that now, knowing the way

she'd died; the girls saw drifts of weed skimming those almond eyes. They felt the ice of death; laughed when they realised that they were still alive.

"I rather liked her," said Maxine generously. (She was such a snob, Maxine liked few people.) "But I guess it leaves a gap now as far as 'A' levels—"

"How can you say that?" cried Ali. "Miss Sagan died last night! I had a dream about it—"

"But we can't bring her back, not from the other side. Miss Sagan's dead and gone."

"How can you be so unkind?"

Maxine shrugged and said, "I'm not being unkind. I'm being rational."

Ali turned away to talk to her other friends. There was a little group of them at one end of the quad. Lynsey and Kate were there, Susie was clinging on – Susie always clung on.

Maxine was Ali's best friend, but she could be a pain; she could be aloof and cool, trapped in her own desires. So slim and elegant that it was hard to believe that she could act like a child. For Maxine was moody, and her looks could be withering; and she had a wicked jealous streak. She could cut others dead, and yet was always there not far from Ali's side. They had a loyal bond which helped them through hard times, and brought them back again if they should drift apart. Of all the friends she'd known, Maxine was generally way ahead in Ali's reckoning.

She was still a pain, though.

Ali nudged at Kate's arm. "You're very quiet on this. Did you like Miss Sagan?"

Kate stared at the lake and sighed, and tossed her flowing hair.

"It wasn't suicide. . . ."

"What do you mean?" said Ali, when she and Kate were alone. "How could you possibly know?"

"I saw her at the lake. I was cutting through the grounds towards the porter's lodge."

"What, in the dead of night?"

Kate's grim face nodded. "I had a rendezvous."

"What kind of rendezvous?"

"More like a lover's tryst. I went to meet someone."

"You went to meet a man?"

Kate slowly nodded again.

"It wasn't an elephant."

They were in the rose arbour in the late afternoon. The long day's rain had passed to leave an autumn sun. They were sitting on a bench hewn out of solid rock. They had their mufflers on.

"Who did you meet?" said Ali, totally stunned by this. The world seemed to have changed before her very eyes. One minute all was clear, laid out in careful lines – and she never realised.

Good grief! Kate met a man, while Miss Sagan had died. The world was full of twists, its roads were vast and wide. And what did Ali do? Sat in her room and dreamed – she felt quite awed by it.

"What kind of man?" she asked.

"Danny, from the riding stables. The one that Mrs Locke took on to help around the school."

"But he found Miss Sagan!"

"I know, it's really weird."

"Did you have sex with him?"

Kate started laughing. "Well, how does that fit in?"

"It's just—" Ali shook her head. "It just seemed obvious. I just thought – late at night, you're out there meeting him – you must have slept with him. What was it like?" she asked.

"I really wouldn't know. I only met him once before last night," said Kate. "We just walked round and talked."

"And that was all you did?" Ali felt her spirits sink. This wasn't so good after all – or maybe yes it was. She fancied him herself; it wouldn't be too good if Kate had slept with him. "But did you kiss him?"

"Well, yes, we kissed," said Kate.

"Then you saw Miss Sagan?"

"No, it was before we met," said Kate. "I was skirting round the lake, and I saw Miss Sagan and Mr Slade arguing."

*She saw Mr Slade*, thought Ali. He was the

English tutor. What would he be doing there? "What time was this?" she asked.

"About half past ten," said Kate.

"And he was with Miss Sagan?"

"They were 'involved'," said Kate. "*You don't know anything!* They've been going around for weeks. You must have known that, Al, they were both really hot."

Ali sat back and sighed. "No, Kate, I never knew."

"You're really dumb," said Kate.

She reached inside her coat pocket and found some Trebor mints, which had been there for a while and were dusted with fluff. She tried to brush it off as two younger girls wandered past, heading towards the school.

It was October now, and leaves were drifting down. The sky had leaden tints, the fields were turning brown. Long lines of flapping geese were heading for the coast. Starlings flew in from town.

"It was kind of embarrassing," Kate murmured thoughtfully. "He was really yelling at her, just in that clump of trees. She was yelling back in French, something about *cochon*. He nearly strangled her."

Kate put the mints away (they weren't worth eating now) and hunched down in her coat, her hands wedged deep inside. She stared through narrowed eyes towards a blood-red sun. Her breath made thin pale clouds.

"It was pretty scary, too. I wasn't supposed to be out – and things weren't going to look too good if they found me out there. So I hid in the trees until they wandered off. But they came back again."

Kate gave a long sigh. "They were really yelling now, and I was backing off, trying to work through the trees to reach the porter's lodge. But I kept looking back, because he had a lump of wood, and was hitting a tree with it. I could see him in the moonlight, just pounding on a tree—"

"You think he murdered her?"

"That's not what I'm saying," said Kate. "It's just that they were there, and he was going berserk, and it was frightening. Miss Sagan rejected him, that's what it sounded like, and he was really mad and said she was a whore. I couldn't quite see that, I mean, Claudine Sagan – she was hardly a whore, was she?"

"But what you're talking about," Ali said under her breath, perched on the edge of the bench, her hands clasped like a vice, "is Mr Slade killing her, and drowning her in the lake—"

"Faking an accident."

A silence settled over the two tense girls as they stayed on the bench inside the damp arbour. The evening sun was warm, but the bench and ground were cold. They felt it in their bones.

# 4

That evening frost touched the ground; the moon was sharp as ice against a jet-black sky, and even darker still, the outline of the school rose up like battlements.

In the third-floor windows of the narrow west wing, above the empty quad where plants died in their beds, the sixth-form lights blazed out like signals to the stars, and sixth-form girls lay down. It was almost lights-out, and the girls were winding down: four girls to each small room, four beds, four chests of drawers. They had a wardrobe each, but they were so confined that coats would barely fit in them.

Alison was sitting on the bedroom window-ledge, looking out across the quad. Sometimes her eyes gazed up to watch the full-blown moon. Her face looked thin and pale, dogged with her weighty thoughts; her eyes looked lost and grave.

She had her uniform on, although she'd ditched her tie, and one black shoe had slipped off as her toes brushed the wall. She might have been quite cold, but was so lost in thought that she seemed unaware.

"Are you going to the bathroom?" asked Lynsey.

"I've already been." Ali's head swivelled round as Lynsey left the room. Maxine had already gone, to check her perfect skin. Ali and Kate were left.

"What are you going to do, then?" she said to Kate, already in bed.

Kate put John Betjeman down, and said, "I couldn't say."

"You ought to tell someone. You ought to tell the police. At least tell Mrs Locke."

Kate lay and stared at her. "And get expelled for it? You know how strict they are about us meeting guys. The two things we can't do are have sex and mess with drugs. You get expelled for it."

"But not in this case," said Ali. "You didn't have any sex." She slid down from the ledge and knelt down on Kate's bed.

"Do you think they'd go for that? I'm out at twelve o'clock – would they think I'm rat-catching?" Kate set her book on the floor. "Remember Paula-Jean? They kicked old Paula out for meeting boys at night. What do you think they'd do with me? Danny is twenty-four. This is not the normal world."

"Write them a letter," said Ali.

"Sure, in my handwriting. They don't want things like that, they need some witnesses. I'll either have to go myself, or we keep quiet about it, which means we never tell. You have to keep it quiet too, Al. We can't go spreading this kind of stuff around. He might be innocent – I only told it to you because you're my best friend."

"I know," said Alison.

"I really mean it, Al. What if she killed herself or had an accident? We can't blame Mr Slade – we all *like* Mr Slade. I can't see him murdering her."

"So you're not going to do anything?" said Ali after a while.

"I don't know," Kate replied. "I don't know what to do. We could be really wrong, and make a whole big mess and end up looking like fools."

They stopped abruptly as Maxine entered the room. She was towelling her damp hair dry; she wore a short night-gown. Even fresh from having a wash she retained her dark, stunning looks. God really liked Maxine.

"What are you two up to?" she said. "You look as thick as thieves."

"Nothing," Ali replied, as she jumped up from Kate's bed.

She started stripping off while Maxine stared at her. And felt some jealousy. . . .

The following morning, through life's coincidence, Ali had an English lesson. It took place in a room in the generally gloomy west wing, directly under the sixth-form bedrooms. But this room was large and bright, with views from two long walls through leaded windows. It wasn't warm though – the boilers had packed up, and the silver frost outside was tapping on the panes. The girls all sat and froze while Mr Slade paced around, trying to stir up some warmth.

Ali was staring hard at him. She couldn't stop staring. She didn't hear his voice, but just stared at his face. Had he killed Miss Sagan? Ali could not believe he had. But Kate had seen him threaten her. Did that mean anything, or was she tossing straws, adding a little spice to the recent tragedy? If she could look through John Slade's eyes would it put a stop to her imaginings?

Things looked very different now in the cold light of day, when every passing hour sent suspicion further back. It seemed too much to believe that death was walking round dressed up in John Slade's clothes. God, he was handsome: she fancied him more than Danny. Nothing so wrong in that, all the girls fancied him. He was so tall and dark, so tanned, his eyes so brown – why wasn't he married yet? Maybe that was it, she thought – had he asked Miss Sagan, and she'd rejected him? It was hardly likely – she hadn't been there long. But then how long did it take to really love someone? How was he feeling now, knowing that his love was dead? And he her murderer. . . .

"Alison?"

Ali jumped. She'd been drifting miles away.

"I said, 'How do you interpret Chaucer's view of the Church?'"

"Erm—" Alison was blank. She glanced down at her book. "I think I missed that one."

"You missed a lot of things," he said.

What did that mean? Was that a hint to her that he'd looked inside her thoughts? Had he read Ali's mind and seen the doubts Kate had planted there, and was he toying with her?

But Mr Slade was smiling at her, which helped to confuse her more. His smile looked real and pure, just like his smile of old. Could that conceal a heart which must be black and cold? Ali could not think so.

"Sorry," she said, "I'm back again," and sat up in the chair and smiled back. Leave this thing to the police, who know what's going on. "Chaucer's new what?" she said.

"What was that all about?" said Maxine later on. "You two were grinning like fools."

"Just one of those things," Ali said.

"I think he fancies you."

"He doesn't fancy me."

"He *really* fancies you." Maxine looked disgusted. "It's really pitiful. Right there in front of the class, you're making big cow eyes. Next thing we know, you'll be sprawled across his desk and we'll be looking on. I think it's sickening."

"What's bitten you?" said Ali as they crossed the quadrangle, their arms crammed full of books, their heels crunching the stone. They both walked double-fast to dodge the threatening rain, which was about to pour on them.

"Nothing's bitten me," Maxine said moodily. "I just think it's really gross the way you were making eyes at him."

"I wasn't 'making eyes'—" said Ali.

"*Someone* was making eyes. You should have been where we were sitting."

The taller girl yanked a heavy door open and stepped into a hallway which ran for almost the entire length of the main school building, more like a corridor. It had high panelled sides and a dark parquet floor. Pictures hung from the walls.

"You've changed a lot," Maxine said underneath her breath, as they ran down the hall towards their next classroom. "You don't have any time for me, now you've got all your new friends around."

"What are you talking about?"

"You and Kate Stone for a start," said Maxine, slowing down as they approached the room where the geography class was held. "You two seem pretty close."

"Just because I talk to her?"

"Why don't you marry her?" Maxine shoved a glass door open and burst into a small room where several girls sat round chatting, perched on the lids of desks. "I thought you were *my* friend."

"I really am your friend!"

"It doesn't look like it."

That was as far as things got then, because Mrs Mullen arrived almost immediately. She came in like a breeze, all frills and bits of lace.

"Good morning, girls," she said.

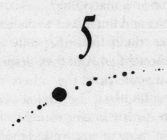

# 5

Maxine's jealousy, like many of her moods, was a fairly intense but relatively short-lived affair, and by the time the weekend came (cold weather from the north) she'd settled down again. Maxine probably couldn't help it, for she'd had it pretty rough when she was very young, when both her parents died and left her to be raised by two aunts in Dorset. That kind of thing can't be easy, especially as both the aunts were in their seventies by then. It was in fact quite an achievement that Maxine had survived as well as she appeared to have done.

By Saturday morning though, her mood had run its course, and she was as beautiful as only she could be. Of all the girls at Summervale she was the one most blessed with looks and elegance. She joined Kate and Lynsey and Ali when they went horse riding. It was the kind of school where it was on the curriculum. Some fenced, some swam, some danced, but Maxine and her friends all knew that the best went horse riding. . . .

Of course Susie Minter had to be there tagging along, because theirs was the only group that would even tolerate her. And they despised the girl, so you can imagine how the others treated her. Poor Susie was hopeless; she couldn't find a friend if everyone on earth was sent round to her door. It was just one of those things; Susie simply had a gift for driving people away.

Being unprepossessing had not advanced her cause, and she had a whining way and a desperate, hungry look. God must have grabbed the last few bits and squeezed them into one – and that's what Susie was.

Her parents were hard up, and she was there on a scholarship, which meant she had the brains which could scare others away. And being so poorly dressed Susie would never be picked as an accoutrement. So Susie tagged along trying to be involved, and laughed at all their jokes and had none of her own. And how she felt inside nobody really knew, because no one talked to her. . . .

The local riding school was less than a kilometre

away from the tall wrought-iron gates which fronted Summervale, along a thin dirt track which was partly overgrown with weeds, overhung by chestnut trees. It was a spooky place to be alone when night descended, for there were only two bare lamps which did not give out much light. But walking in a group, on a bright autumn day, there was not much to worry about.

The view was open, with fields on either side, and rabbits in the wheat-chaff reapers left behind. Kestrels flew overhead, clouds capped blue distant hills – this was a peaceful day. But the girls' topic of conversation was still the main one that had engrossed the school for almost all that week. Though it at least appeared that the death of Miss Sagan had been fully explained. . . .

"Well, the way I heard it," Lynsey said assertively, "and I got this one practically straight from the horse's mouth, was that there was a big bruise on the side of her face, which they think she may have got when she slipped on the landing stage, and then she hit her head against one of the wooden piles and rolled off into the lake. She must have been unconscious even before she hit the water."

"Thank goodness for that," muttered Ali; it was a relief to know that Mr Slade was not involved, though it seemed a little bizarre to come out with a sigh of relief on finding out how Miss Sagan died.

Maxine said, "But what I want to know is, what was she doing there at that time of night? It was a filthy night and it was pouring down – what was she, crazy? She was last seen inside the main school building just after ten o'clock – so what did she do then? I mean – what? At twelve o'clock she goes down to the lake? What was she doing there?"

"Well, they couldn't ask her – they can't know everything." Lynsey just gave a shrug to show she didn't care, and used her riding crop to slash the dense nettles which grew along the track.

"Actually," Susie said quietly, "there is more to the story than that. I heard it yesterday." Then she seemed to bite her tongue, as if slightly alarmed that she had spoken out.

The four girls turned to look at her. She was always one step behind. Always just on the fringe, never fully involved.

She said, "They were just assuming she'd slipped, although they couldn't find any evidence that she'd fallen on the landing stage. There were no skin traces or little flecks of blood – which they would have expected to find if she'd landed on a pile. There was nothing there at all, and so they just surmised that was what happened to her."

"How do you know all that?" Lynsey asked warily, as just for once in her life Susie had them on the hook.

She said, "I was in the hall and heard two police officers talking in the corridor."

"But it was raining hard the night that Miss Sagan died—"

Susie just smiled and shrugged. "They should still find something."

"Well, there's a mystery," said Maxine, after a thoughtful pause while all the girls digested Susie's piece of news. "A full-blown mystery."

"But they still closed the file on her," Susie offered cheerfully.

"Danny?" Ali was in a stall with Max, her four-year-old grey cob, looking at Danny's back as he reached underneath the horse to grab the canvas girth. The light was soft in the stable, with tiny motes of dust which made a sepia hue. The air was hot and musty with the smell of the horse, and crushed straw underfoot.

"What was it like when you found her?"

Danny paused for a moment – then buckled up the girth. His hair fell in his face, his hands stroked Max's mane. He took a short step back and looked into her face. "What did she look like?"

Ali nodded. She couldn't stop thinking about it. About how Miss Sagan must have looked lying in the water, her body stiff and pale, death in her final gaze. "Did she look cold and grey?"

He stared straight in her eyes. "You shouldn't think about it."

*It was he who found her lying amongst the reeds. Who saw her empty eyes and sensed the smell of death. It was he who sprinted back to advise Mrs Locke. It was he who touched her face.*

"I can't stop thinking about it."

"She was very cold," he said. "But she'd been dead for a while, and it was a freezing night. She could have been fast asleep – except her eyes were wide, and she was floating in a lake."

He turned away from Ali to unbolt the door of the stall, pushing the horse away as it tried to nuzzle his neck. His face was lean and tanned, his eyes as dark as coals. "I tried to pull her out."

Danny was a mystery; nobody knew his past. He worked at the riding school and helped out at Summervale. He helped old Mr Potts, the ancient gardener. He did odd jobs around. He was very dark skinned, which gave him a gypsy look, and his hair was long and brown and feathered round his neck. They said that he could break a horse in just by touching it. His slim body was tough and strong.

"Did you meet Kate?" she asked.

He turned and grinned at her, with a shy but piercing grin which almost stalled her breath. It probed right in her soul and made her heart beat fast. He said, "Kate's very young."

Ali let her breath ease out and turned towards her horse. She stroked him on the neck, and checked the bridle's fit. The air felt close and still, the stall's scent warm and thick.

"Am I too young as well?"

She could sense Danny's presence behind her – the silence of the stall, the muted sounds beyond. She felt the horse's breath, warm on her own bare neck – she felt her shaking heart. She was amazed that she'd dared to ask him that, had voiced her own attraction and gone behind Kate's back. But most of all she felt a real and deep desire that he should like her, too.

"Am I too forward?"

She couldn't look at him, dared not brave Danny's gaze in case this was a mistake. Yet she felt him drawing near, his strong hands on her arms. And Kate yelled *"Are you ready yet?"*

The world came back again as Danny stepped away, and Ali felt raging flames tear through her pounding heart. She had never kissed someone, had never held them close.

"This is not my day," she sighed.


"What do you think, then?" Kate whispered, after lights out that evening. "Do you think he still likes me?"

Filled with guilt, Ali could not say anything.

"We didn't actually make a date or anything, but he still looks at me as though he's keen on me. What do you think?" said Kate, as she sat up in her bed. "Are you awake over there?"

"I'm awake," Ali murmured.

"I am, too," Maxine chipped in. "Who are we talking about?"

"Danny Morrisey."

"Oh, from the riding school." There was a rustle of bedclothes as Maxine sat up, prepared to talk for a while. "What about him?"

"I think he's really cute. Couldn't you just die for him?"

Ali rolled onto her side, and stared out through the gap between the thick curtains which never closed properly no matter how they tugged or tried to fix them up. The night looked moonless and solid, a sheet of total black beyond the window-pane. No light touched it at all. No sound came from outside, save for a poacher's gun.

# 6

The next morning Ali was very quiet, and felt like being alone. It was a Sunday, and they had the day to themselves, but the girls were usually bored. Ali went for a walk around the empty grounds. She had a thick coat on. She really needed it, for the day was freezing. Small clouds of snowy white steamed from her tight, pale lips. Thick frost lay underfoot and grass crunched like thin ice. The ground felt hard as rock.

Her mind was spinning, and she couldn't work things out – the guilt and thrill and fear that Danny brought to her. If it had not been for Kate she would not have found the nerve to make a pass at him. If Kate could do it, then why couldn't she do it? Ali had spoken out to let him know how she felt. It hadn't been planned that way, it just seemed to occur. It just seemed natural. But what was Kate going to say, and how was she going to feel if Ali said that she thought Danny wanted her? It was a dirty deed, but one she couldn't change even if someone forced her to. Because she really liked him, and had always fancied him, though never really thought she stood a chance with him. Maybe she'd got it wrong, but somehow Ali sensed that Danny liked her, too.

So where did Kate stand? Was she going to be over the moon? *For heaven's sake, Ali, how are you going to handle this?* Ali had no idea, and all that she could think was that she wanted him. . . .

She walked towards the lake, as people were prone to do because the grass sloped down into a natural dip. The lake was silver-still; no coots moved on its face, no herons stalked its shore. The day was dazzling, and no clouds lay in the sky, which was straight cobalt blue with a low blinding sun. Tree-tops were sharp and clear monochrome silhouettes. The distant hills were blue.

Ali stopped and stared at them. The hills were always blue, and she couldn't work that out – what were they, iron ore? When it rained they disappeared as if shrinking into the ground. What people lived out there? She sensed the school behind her, like a brooding grey-skinned beast, a monstrous knot of stone clawing the sky. She could feel its every thought directed at her back; its thick-glass hundred eyes.

She turned to look at it. Who had created the place? Who built those roofs and spires, those soaring campaniles? Summervale was an eerie place, made up of many styles. Who had *liked* the place?

There were other girls walking some way across the field, and Ali quickly turned away and stepped down to the shore. Two long thin lines of frozen reeds stretched out. Bulrushes waved their spears. A fox barked quite close by.

She stood on the landing stage, the reeds to either side, the silver lake ahead, the boathouse on her left. She could smell burning leaves from Potts's latest fire. Sunlight lanced her eyes. She pulled her coat tight, her hands wrapped in blue gloves, her orange woollen scarf looped round her almost frozen neck. If it was like this now, what was it going to be like when the winter months arrived?

Her breath came steaming out, almost burning her nose, and her blue eyes squinted tight against the blazing sun. She was staring ahead to where a figure stood, watching the water. He seemed oblivious to the cold which gripped the day, his long tan coat pushed back by the hands in his trouser pockets. His grey suit jacket was undone, his shirt was rucked at the waist, his tie was slightly awry.

The man was looking at the water as if he'd

dropped something into it, and was debating the best way of getting it out again. He seemed unaware that she stood watching, wrapped up in his own private daydream. But without any warning he suddenly spoke to her.

"It's a very cold day," he said softly. "Cold on the fish. Can't be too much fun down there." His long face turned towards her, offering a pleasant smile beneath his silver hair. He was in his late forties, and had wide-set grey eyes which made him look benign. "Are there any fish in here?"

"I don't really know," she said. "I would suppose so." She hugged her upper arms and took a nervous step, shifting her weight from one foot to the other. "You're Inspector Blair," she said. It was a half-question.

"And you are?"

"Alison."

The Inspector nodded as if he already knew that, though it hardly seemed likely since the school was full of girls. "Do you get Sundays off?"

"It's our most boring day. We don't have much to do."

The Inspector nodded thoughtfully, as if he understood. He seemed the kind of man people would talk to. He didn't say too much, but seemed quite at his ease. He didn't press people.

"I was going for a walk," she said. "To get away from things."

He smiled. "Do your friends get too much when they're there all the time?"

Ali smiled back ruefully. "I guess a little bit. Sometimes you need to be on your own."

"I know what you mean," said Blair as he slowly looked away, gazing back at the lake as though it troubled him.

Ali followed his languid look, stared at the cold, still depths. Miss Sagan was found just there.

"Is that what you're looking for?" she asked. "A further clue?"

"A clue to what?" said Blair, his smile half-curious.

"I heard that you should have found some clues – like bits of skin and things." She glanced down at the mossy wooden piles with some reluctance.

Inspector Blair shrugged his shoulders. "No, I think we're satisfied about what happened that night. I was just having a last look round, trying to round things off. I suppose I have the kind of mind that doesn't like to leave loose ends. But it's not important."

"It's kind of creepy," Ali said, shivering; her eyes drawn to the spot where she thought the fall might have occurred.

Blair put his hand on her waist and gently steered her away.

"Let's go back to the school," he said.

# 7

The next week passed by quietly, with the memory of Miss Sagan gradually drifting away, until by the time the weekend came it was scarcely possible to believe it had happened. Life returns to normal as soon as possible, as people can't survive with nightmares in their head. It is a human trait which enables the rest of the world to surmount tragedies.

Susie Minter had a hard week, though that wasn't unusual because she usually did. Lynsey in particular was very hard on her. Lynsey detested her. For the rest of the girls, though, life was as usual, with all the petty things which make life tough or fun. Maxine cried at her spots, Ali saw two hedgehogs, Kate's chest filled out again. Mr

Slade took up jogging, which made a lot of the girls want to start jogging, too. Mr Bleak had two days' sick; Mrs Day came over faint; Mrs Locke re-styled her hair.

All in all, this was life at Summervale; a place set on its own, a well-heeled microcosm. While the wide world heaved and throbbed, turned itself this way and that, time here meandered on.

Kate was restless all week, though, because she had a desperate urge to be near Danny again and moon into his eyes. It was all the others could do to stop her climbing the fence and sprinting across the fields. Which didn't do Ali much good, for she was yearning too, but could not swoon and sigh as openly as Kate. She had to keep things to herself, and found that guilt and lies make painful bedfellows.

She was half-dreading going back to the riding school, not knowing how Danny would look, or whether Kate was going to suspect. Yet above all else she was on tenterhooks, aching to get there. Why did it all have to be so difficult? Why couldn't Kate fall ill? Why couldn't she stay behind? If only just this once something would happen to Kate, to keep her out of the way.

But by the time Sunday morning came (their normal weekly class had had to be rearranged, to accommodate a gymkhana which occupied the riding school most of the Saturday) Kate was really bubbling, with all the fear and thrill that only crushes bring. She could not stay sat still, she could not clean her teeth for putting eye make-up on.

Ali's heart plummeted as she watched her friend prepare, knowing that she herself was trying to look her best. She had tied her long hair back, thinking it looked more mature. She'd put pale lipstick on.

"Are you nearly ready yet?"

"I'm nearly ready," said Ali, though she could have done with another hour at least before she'd feel her best. She wanted to say that Kate was rushing her and making Ali tense – but she still felt too ashamed. Besides which, it would not look too cool to turn out all dolled up right at the crack of dawn.

"We'd better go," said Kate as Ali gave a sigh and put her make-up down.

"*Katie!*" said Maxine. "It's only half-past nine, we've got ages yet."

Kate pulled an anguished face. "But I'm all ready now. We can go and help out at the riding school until eleven o'clock."

"Or we can simply take our time the way we normally do, and not go raving mad." Maxine rolled her dark eyes, and took a silver brush and slowly ran it through her shining raven hair. It could take Maxine most of a day to get prepared sometimes, and she was not going to start rushing now.

Poor Kate sat down in frustration amongst the battlefield that their former bedroom had been transformed into. There was make-up everywhere; heaps of assorted clothes; their well-worn riding gear. But she couldn't stay still, and went wandering downstairs, while Ali felt her tension squirming deep inside. She *would* see Danny soon, and for all her nerves and guilt that was what mattered most. . . .

Poor Susie Minter was hanging round again, looking on hopefully. Susie's parents could not afford to buy her a horse of her own, or pay for riding lessons, so Susie generally stood around watching the other girls and helping them get prepared.

The girls were not insensitive to this unhappy fact, despite the things they said when Susie's back was turned, but short of sharing a horse with her there wasn't much they could do, save to let her lend a hand. And to be truthful Susie did not seem to mind too much, although sometimes they caught her staring hard at them. If they had thought to look, and stared down deep inside, they must have seen how much it hurt. . . .

On that fateful morning it was Ali's turn to have Susie helping her. Susie was on her tiptoes, sorting out the horse's mane. She said, "You're very quiet."

"I've got a lot on my mind."

"Have you seen Kate over there, glued onto Danny's side?"

"Maybe she fancies him."

"I think she must do," said Susie cheerfully, pulling the last strap tight, tugging the stirrups down. "Your Max is really great."

Ali climbed on his back. "Yes, isn't he?" she said.

Ali turned the horse away and walked Max into the yard, his new shoes clattering across the cobbled ground. The grey's breath snorted out as though he'd just woken up, and was not geared up for this. They stood and waited for the others, watching the to and fro of the ever busy yard. The indoor school loomed up, huge and black at their backs. The sun shone. Stall doors slammed.

"Hi there. Are you ready?" said Lynsey, as she weaved her bay, Sovereign, past a pile of useless tack someone had dumped on the ground. Ali tried her best to respond, but found her attention fixed on Danny chatting with Kate.

He was thirty metres away, deep in conversation. He had been there all this time, and not once looked Ali's way. And Kate was smiling back, like she was Danny's girl. And waving across at her. But then Danny turned her way, and right there, suddenly, Ali saw Danny change, saw the longing in his gaze. And for all Kate's brave attempts, Ali sensed there and then that he was meant for her.

She sat there motionless as a soft smile wreathed his face. His eyes were two dark flames which burned into her own. She felt her stuttering heart, the heaving of her breast. Silence surrounded her.

Then it was over, and he was coming towards her, his brown eyes on her face, Kate watching puzzledly. His shoulder touched her leg as he checked on Max's girth. He whispered, "You look great."

Ali could hardly speak to him, her voice froze in her throat. She felt on fire inside, her heart punched at her ribs. He said, "I need some help to brush the horses down."

"I could come back later on." Ali just breathed the words.

He said, "I hoped you would."

"Hey! What is this, then? I thought we'd paid for this—" Maxine's voice intervened, but not ill-naturedly. "Are we going for a ride, or what?"

Danny took one step back. "Good luck. And have good fun."

The four girls moved off, though Kate lingered at the rear, trying to understand the sudden change that appeared to have taken place. The whole day had been turned around, so that all at once it seemed Danny had drifted away. She didn't know why this was, and she couldn't understand, though it left her hurt and sad to sense his feelings alter.

She stared at Ali's back, and wondered what she had that Kate herself did not.

Standing quietly observing all this was Susie Minter, who always watched them leave with a calm look on her face. If Susie ached inside at being left behind, she never let them see. . . .

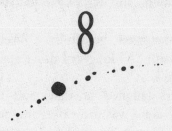

# 8

They went down the lane to the left of the riding school; across a muddy track which led up to a farm. One of the school dogs was at their heels, its tongue trailing the ground. It often came when they rode out. There was some tension in the air, though only Ali knew what was the cause of it. Her three friends sensed that something had happened, but didn't quite know what.

In an attempt to break the mood Lynsey reined in her horse, half way up a stony track between two hedge-lined fields. In the distance woodsmoke curled from a crowded, gloomy copse. In the hedge a pheasant called. As she patted Sovereign's neck Lynsey said, "Danny said that maybe once in a while we ought to change around and swap our horses."

"What for?" said Maxine.

"To ride a different horse, for more experience. He said we're becoming lazy because we can all handle our own, and we ought to try something new."

Maxine shrugged gracefully. "Well, I don't mind," she said. "As long as I don't get that stupid lump of Kate's."

The others laughed at that, and the tension slipped away. Kate was too easy-going to stay upset for long. She simply laughed and shrugged. *Maybe another time. Maybe with someone else.*

They all dismounted in front of the metal gate which led into the field where they normally galloped out. The horses pushed and shoved and one stood on Maxine's foot. She gave a startled yelp. But finally it got sorted out – and Kate was riding Max. Ali had Kate's old horse, and Lynsey took Sultan. Maxine seemed a little miffed that she'd had to swap Sultan for Lynsey's lazy bay. She was also a little hurt by the fact that she and Lynsey had swapped, when she'd assumed she would have changed with Alison. They were the two best friends, so that seemed logical.

Jealousy bit again.

But before Maxine could say anything, Kate opened up the gate and led Max into the field, and let the others through. She shoved the stiff gate back and went to climb on Max. The grey took one step back.

"Oh come here, Max," she muttered, and tried again, and got as far as putting her left foot in the stirrup. Max seemed a little tense, and was pawing at the ground. He was eyeing her nervously. "What's the matter with him?" she said as she pulled up off the ground, and found for a startled moment that Max was pawing air. Kate just had time to gasp before Max thundered off. She was not on him yet. . . .

The horse went crazy, he was really travelling; no one had ever seen him move so fast before. The other horses spooked as he went tearing past. They all struggled to hold them back. Max seemed demented as Kate clung to his side. His eyes were wide and white, his tongue dripped flecks of foam. He tried to throw some bucks into his gallop stride. Kate crouched, just off the ground. And the ground was flashing past as Max raced up the hill, filled with a fear and rage which was aimed at Kate. The horse had just one thought: to get Kate off his back – to kill her if he could.

The girl could feel it – two tonnes of grey fury which seemed intent on wreaking some great harm on her. This horse would break her neck; this horse would crush her bones. Kate could see it in his eyes. She could hear the other girls calling out to her, but they were too far away to be of any help. They were just distant shapes – this was between her and Max. And Max was winning.

There was a jump ahead – a log at the top of the hill which they would usually take at no more than a trot. But Max was bearing down on it at full gallop. There was no chance he would make his stride. Max hurtled into it. He really tried to fly. He gave a massive leap which flung Kate from his back. As she crashed on her spine, she thought she'd killed herself.

The world screamed, then turned black. . . .

# 9

It was in subdued mood that they all led their mounts back to the riding school. Kate hadn't killed herself, but she'd come very close. Her entire body ached and her lungs felt on fire. It seemed a long slow walk as she limped down the lane, as if she'd dropped from an aeroplane.

"What on earth happened?" said Danny, as he ran out to meet them in the lane.

"Max just went mad," said Maxine. "He went tearing off and we had an awful job trying to get him back again. He was stamping on the ground and trying to bite us all—"

"So what got into him?"

"I don't know," said Ali, holding on to Kate, who looked prepared to drop and slump down in the road. "He didn't act like Max."

"I think I'm going to be sick," Kate mumbled dismally.

"We'd better get you back to school," said Danny, taking over. He lifted Kate gently in his arms and walked her through the yard towards his battered car, which was parked underneath a tree. "The rest of you had better come with me, too. Just put your horses in the stalls and leave them there for now. I'll sort them out later. . . ."

It was only later, when he examined Max, that Danny found the piece of barbed wire wedged underneath the girth.

He had to prise it out from Max's bloody flank.

You couldn't blame the horse.

# 10

As to how it got there, that was a matter open to some conjecture. The general feeling was that Max must have picked it up by brushing against the fence when Kate led him through the gate. This left questions unanswered, but with Kate in a state of shock, there wasn't time for them. They were all just so relieved that she'd managed to walk away with nothing more severe than minor cuts and bumps. Kate had been shaken up, but wasn't about to die, as at first she'd feared she might.

The school nurse examined her in the tiny sick bay. (Mrs Fay Paladine, built like a stack of bricks. A woman like a man, with a moustache on her lip, and hands like coal shovels.) She said nothing was broken. Kate would recover, and there was no need for her to go to hospital. But Kate felt very weak and spent a lousy day draped in an armchair.

She didn't miss much; the weather in the afternoon turned grim, bringing brutal storms with rain like fusillades. By the time evening came the world was black as pitch, and the school was shivering. . . .

The rain was still lashing at Summervale's windows as the hour neared midnight. The school was flinching from the tempest's onslaught; a fortress under siege from the howling wind outside. Doors rattled in their frames, curtains billowed out like ghosts, strained timbers creaked and groaned. No one was moving, for most of the school was asleep. The darkened classrooms stood like empty mausoleums. Textbooks lay out on desks as if reading themselves. Tall blackboards preached alone.

On the high third storey of the gloomy west wing, where the sixth-form girls were settled, tucked up in their beds, the only sign of life was the fluorescent lights, which blazed to brave the night. They were on in the bathroom, which was at the end of a long dark hall, some twenty metres past the room that Kate shared with her friends. Light showed around the door like a thin dawn leaking out. Pale tendrils touched the walls.

Inside the room, with its rows of dull white tiles, Kate revelled in the bath she'd been allowed to run.

She should have been in bed, but to compensate for her day she had been granted this. It was a special privilege, permitted just this once by Mr Slade, who was the tutor on duty that night. She'd filled the bathtub up with every scent she had, and wallowed in its warmth. It was a special luxury to hear the wind outside, while she soaked up to her chin in mounds of steaming foam. Her arms hung over the sides, and the rattling of windows in their frames only helped Kate feel more secure.

She had her eyes shut, and her aches were settling down as the water eased her bruising, soothed her cuts and bumps. Her thoughts had hardly turned towards the cruel barbed wire which had put her in this state. How did it get there? Who was responsible? Had it been meant for her or for Ali? These thoughts were just beginning to surface in Kate's mind, when the door came creaking back. . . .

She didn't look around as footsteps crossed the floor; it was probably one of her friends coming in to check on her. It would more than likely be Alison, who had seemed the most concerned. She said, "Is that you, Al?"

Nobody answered, but a shadow touched the wall, and a freezing blast of air came through the open door. It made the bubbles hiss on the surface of the foam. Shivers ran down Kate's arm. She struggled to sit up while she rubbed the sweat from her eyes, and reached for the orange towel she'd hung behind the door. She was about to wipe her face when the hand of Death reached out, and dragged the breath from her.

Kate went out screaming, kicking up clouds of foam. She woke the whole west wing with cries which drowned the storm. They were her words of death which, at the very end, sounded like *Help me*. But no one could help Kate, for she was electrocuted, killed by her own hair dryer being tossed into the bath. And for all the world it looked, to the unsuspecting eye, like a stupid, sad accident.

It was only later, much later, that rumours of murder began to circulate. And before then the whole of Summervale was gripped by mourning. . . .

# 11

*K*ate is dead now. Dead because of an accident. And *I am lonely.*

Ali could not believe it – it was too difficult for her to comprehend. Words from the morning hymn kept running through her mind – *And I am far from home.*

Far from home, she thought. Lonely. Far from the home she loved and all the things she knew. Where were her mother and father? Where was the stupid cat, the posters on her wall?

*I am far from home. And I am lonely.*

It just didn't seem possible. Even when Mrs Locke came round with Mr Slade in tow – breaking the awful news – their eyes all red and bruised—

*I feel so far from home.*

That was what the hymn kept on saying. How did it go now? She was trying to remember it. . . .

*The night is dark, and I am far from home.*
*Lead thou me on.*

What did that mean, though? Who was going to lead her on? Was it death they were talking about?

Of course they'd all known that there was something wrong – you didn't scream like that unless something was *really* wrong. But they thought Kate had just been sick, or had a dream or a fall – they didn't think she'd died. Even when they took her away, they thought she was simply going to the county hospital. They were told to go back to bed and that everything was fine.

And everything *was* fine, until suddenly it was eight-thirty, and Ali thought – "*Eight-thirty?*"

They'd been given a lie-in, which was unusual. The place seemed very quiet, like the school was still asleep. The classrooms were asleep, the boilers were asleep, the teachers were asleep. Nothing was moving, not even the lawn mowers – and Mr Potts got up before the crack of dawn. Even the birds seemed quiet and would not sing their songs.

Then Mrs Locke came round.

She never visited the girls' bedrooms or the room

where they had breakfast. They never saw her face until she reached the stage during Assembly.

And her hair was so perfect—

And she wore a plain black dress with a choker at the throat. The make-up on her handsome face was so subtle and precise that it could have been applied by a professional. But her eyes, though, her red eyes, like she'd been rubbing them, as if they troubled her. And Mr Slade behind, with the same look on his face – no, even worse than hers. She was trying so hard then to keep her dignity, while – what was Mr Slade doing? Just kind of standing there, his strong face creased with lines they'd never seen before, but with the same sad eyes.

And they knew then that something terrible had happened – something so bad and real they did not want to hear.

But she was telling them, and she kept telling them, there had been an accident.

*What kind of accident?*

Kate had died in the bath—

*You must be kidding us, you must – that can't be real.*

But Kate died in the bath. She'd had an accident. Alone and far from home.

It wasn't until the morning's extended Assembly that it really dawned on Ali that this was happening. Kate really was dead – you could feel it in the air, the sense of shock and grief, the pain of dis-belief. When girls began to sob, and half the school joined in – that was when Ali knew.

When she looked up and saw them on the stage – the teachers in their gowns, the tension in their eyes – and when she saw Mr Bleak without his thin brown coat – then Ali really knew.

The staff were standing. The school was starting to stand. Ali rose to her feet as Mrs Locke walked in. And the terrible, awful thing when her chair was not in place, and a moment's panicking. . . .

The embarrassment as Clegg the caretaker, who in the general confusion of the hour had forgotten to place the chair, came rushing from the wings and – the chair scraped on the floor – and Mrs Locke stood there. She looked so brave and so lonely. Not one face in the hall was turned away from her. In a silence so intense that surely no one breathed, they waited for her lead. Because if she broke they all broke, and there were two recent deaths that they all had to survive. It was on Mrs Locke that everyone depended now, and she didn't let them down.

She spoke very quietly – in a voice so soft that many of those at the back strained to hear – "This school has a tradition of rising above moments of adversity. We will be honouring Kate if we uphold that now, and do not yield to our pain. Kate is still in our hearts, and her courageous spirit is bright in Summervale. She is in every heart, and in every word we say we shall remember her. . . ."

# 12

*I'll remember*, thought Ali. *I'll remember her. How can I ever forget her? It was my fault that Danny dropped her. It was me who thought how useful it would be if something happened to her. It was my horse that Kate was riding – he didn't bolt when I was on his back. There wasn't any barbed-wire fence for Max to brush against – they'll think I put it there. I never wanted this, it wasn't my idea. I only want Kate back, with all her hopes and dreams. I want to see her bursting in with her long hair spilling out, all wild and out of control.*

She was in an empty room at the end of the science block, tormenting herself with the kind of guilty thoughts we have when people close to us die. White curtains were billowing in from the windows at her back. Voices came in from outside.

She was at a grey metal desk. There were a dozen of them scattered around the room. They looked too small to be of any practical use, but they were supporting her now. She had her hands locked, for they were shaking so much. Her hair hung round her face in lazy disarray. Her face looked small and pale, dark shading round her eyes where she had rubbed at them.

*I'll never live again, this is the end of things. I'm stuck here all alone and they've abandoned me. My parents aren't around when I really need them. I'm trapped at Summervale.*

Ali looked up as someone came into the room. Mr Slade had been passing by and glanced in through the door. He had seen her sitting there, so lost and all alone, and came in to comfort her. He looked as though he could do with a little comforting himself, though. His face looked tired and strained, his clothes in need of a press. But he put a brave face on, and offered her a smile. "Stuck here all on your own?" he said.

Ali tried to respond, but it didn't really work. Her face felt too worn out to force a smile. She simply looked at him as he walked through the room and sat in front of her.

"It's very hard," he said, rubbing his face in his hands. "It's hard to know what to do or say at an awful time like this. Were you here thinking about her?"

Ali gave a short nod, and her bottom lip quivered.

"Yes, I know," said Mr Slade. "It's very diffi-cult." His voice was dull and slow, as if it was weighed down by weariness, and though he tried to concentrate his eyes seemed vague and lost, and not quite in the world. "There's nothing wrong with that," he murmured. "We have to think of her, or it would be as if she didn't matter—"

"But she did matter," Ali said quietly.

"Yes, I know," he said.

"It all seems so wrong somehow – she didn't do anything, she didn't hurt anyone. Everyone liked her—"

"And that makes it seem meaningless."

Ali nodded. "It all seems meaningless." Her eyes were as raw and lost as Mr Slade's eyes were, and like his they stared into a distant space, a dark and lonely place.

Mr Slade watched her with concern. It was very hard for him to find the words to ease her pain. He said, "It isn't meaningless, for it's only we who are sad, and Kate was never sad. She wasn't sad at the end, and she isn't hurting now, she's not in any pain—"

"We have the pain for her."

"That's right," said Mr Slade. "We have the pain

of friends. But Kate herself had a happy life, and we have to carry on and try to remember that."

"But she's dead now." Ali's face turned to him, looking straight in his eyes as if to seek something. "So what does it all mean? Does God despise us all?"

"I don't know, Alison." He couldn't say more than that, for death is always hard, and seldom logical. It was as hard for him to cope as it was for Alison. But he had to help her out.

He said, "I once read a book about a man whose life at first seemed meaningless. His name was Charles de Foucault. He was a Frenchman, an engineer or something. At about the turn of the century he had a feeling that he was wasting his life, and could do better with it, do things to help people, to find a different way. So he took himself off to the Sahara – a cave in Algeria, or some harsh place like that – and he set up a kind of spiritual retreat where people could go to learn about their own spirit. It was just a dream that he'd had, about a way of life that gave things back to the world. And people came to him – though they never stayed for long, and drifted away again."

Ali glanced round as somewhere a door banged. But it was a fleeting thing, and the world seemed still and calm. The voices had faded away, the curtains were rustling, with a sound like butterfly wings.

"And one day he was murdered," Mr Slade continued. "By a gang of thieves."

That wasn't quite what Ali had been expecting. Was this a cheery tale? Was it supposed to lift her up? It was more like misery, like he was encouraging her to plunge into despair.

"At that point," Mr Slade said, "the man's life appeared like a total failure, and it would be hard to find something that, to the rest of us, could seem more meaningless. But about ten years after the murder, when his diaries and writings were discovered, other people began to pay attention to the vision that Brother Charles had. It gave them comfort and inspiration, and gave a meaning to their own confusing lives, and all across the world people began to live their lives by the principles he formed. They are out there now, working quietly in inner cities and run-down housing estates. Just trying to help people less fortunate than themselves. All without fanfare.

"So maybe it wasn't entirely meaningless. We can't tell at the time what good is going to emerge—"

Ali stared hard at him. "But it was a hair dryer. A stupid hair dryer. . . ."

# 13

Later that day, though, rumours began to circulate about the so-called accident. They started quietly, as many rumours do, with half-imagined things that began to take shape. They started with whispering, which then accelerated to a raucous babbling.

The initial assumption had been that Kate, who must have been confused and not thinking clearly, perhaps a little concussed after her fall from Max's back, had made the fatal mistake of taking her hair dryer into the bathroom with her. It was plugged into a long extension cable, which in turn was plugged into a socket in the outer hallway. She must have foolishly tried drying her hair with it, while sitting in the bath. . . .

The rumours, though, added a grain of doubt to this, and began of all places with Clegg the caretaker – a man who normally seemed to just put rubbish out, and shift the chairs around.

Clegg did not live on the school's premises, but down in the town with his wife and brood of dogs, and it was only because of the storm that he'd returned to Summervale late on that evening. For although he was a surly and introverted man, who must have been born with the permanent scowl he wore, Clegg took great pride in his work and battled ceaselessly to keep things functioning. . . .

Rain was lashing and doors were banging as Mr Clegg strove to repair a gushing leak in the flooded boiler room. He had complained in the past that the school was prone to leaks, and though Mrs Locke agreed with him nothing was ever done. He was cursing under his breath as water streamed down his neck and swirled around his feet.

He left the boiler room to check the guttering, peering up through the gloom at the west wing's towering walls. He held an old flashlight whose beam poked through the night with the power of a candle flame.

Water was cascading down Summervale's ancient stones. Thick Boston ivy hissed as the wind's hands tore at it. Phone wires sang in the night like banshees of the storm. Clegg almost lost his footing.

It was well past eleven o'clock by then, and the storm had reached its peak. Clouds were stacked up like hills, pouring down across the world. Wind smacked around his face and flapped his waxed grey coat. His hands were frozen stiff.

A length of ivy whipped back and hit his face, and as Clegg stepped back a pace he dropped the torch on the path. As he stooped to pick it up he sensed a light come on in the gloom above his head. Someone had entered the sixth-form bathroom. It was the time that Kate had gone to take her bath. Of course Clegg didn't know about that and scarcely bothered to look; he had enough on his plate. A few minutes later, though, as he shone the torch again, trying to locate the spot from which the worst of the water came, it flashed into the gloom of the sixth-form corridor, and Clegg saw a figure move.

It was there for an instant, a passing fleeting shape, which didn't mean a thing to him in those circumstances. It was only later on, when Kate had been found dead, that he began to think on it. Maybe she wasn't alone that night; it could be that someone else had crept along the gloom of the silent corridor. Someone who had a plan to get Kate out of there—

Preferably stone cold dead. . . .

# 14

The fear and confusion brought on by this new idea emerged in many ways. When Ali went to her room that night she found a blazing row was taking place in it. The rage came from Lynsey's lips, and the stunned recipient was Lynsey's pet *bête noire*. Lynsey had a thing about Susie Minter, and tried to pick on her as often as she could. Maybe it had something to do with their backgrounds and families, for Susie's was very proud of her, where Lynsey's seemed to neglect her. Whatever the reason was, with her nerves at breaking point, it wasn't hard to find a cause to fight.

Susie had heard a rumour (the second of the day) that just before she died Kate called out someone's name. Some said it wasn't clear, but others said that Kate had called out *"Mr Slade!"*

Whether this was a plea for help, or a cry to ward him off was a cause of great debate amongst the rumour-group. But as far as Lynsey was concerned it was a chance to let off steam, and scald Susie with it.

"And what would you know?" she started scornfully. "No one would talk to you 'cause you're a little creep. You're always hanging round, and if it wasn't for you Kate might not even be dead."

The accusation caught Susie off guard, and, like Ali, she wasn't sure what Lynsey was talking about. But Lynsey certainly knew, even if she was a little confused by her own anguish and grief.

She said, "If it wasn't for you there would never have been an accident, and she wouldn't have even been in the bath."

"What are you talking about?" Susie said, puzzled, fingering her spectacles frame and trying not to flush too much.

"I mean it's very strange that the barbed wire stuck into Max, when there wasn't any barbed wire around." This was a fact that had puzzled many of the girls, and Lynsey thought she'd finally found an answer for it. "But you were hanging round, and helping Al tack-up – what a strange coincidence."

"But why should I do it?" said Susie, backing off as Lynsey looked as though she might lay into her.

"Because you're a little creep and we all wish you were dead, and Kate was popular."

"Then I would have done it to Kate's horse—"

"No, you're too clever for that." Lynsey's voice hissed with scorn. It spat out like a snake. "You probably heard Danny saying that we should swap the horses round, and so you planned for that. Because it's funny that nothing happened while we were walking down the lane – it was only when Kate climbed up when we were inside the field. I've got it all worked out – you slipped the barbed wire into place when Ali was already on his back. It would just be twitching him then, it wouldn't be bothering him – it was only the weight of Kate when she pulled up off the ground—"

"Oh, that's ridiculous!"

"Don't call me ridiculous!" Lynsey took a sudden swipe.

Susie jumped back and landed on Kate's bed.

Lynsey's dark eyes flashed as she leapt across the room and dragged Susie off the bed. "Get off that bed!" she hissed. "That's what it was all along! You wanted Kate's place – you sleazy little creep." There was a definite viciousness about Lynsey at that point, and both Susie and Ali could see that she was poised to fight. If there'd been a weapon to hand she would have picked it up. She had an insane rage.

"I could really kill you." The voice was soft and low. It was as cold as ice, like a sharp blade in the night. Against the dark backcloth of the window at her back, Lynsey looked maniacal. Her eyes were blazing and her dark hair hung in sheets. Her slim hands turned to claws as she braced herself to fight. Her breath was panting out – spittle was on her cheek. Her grief had turned to rage.

"Get out of here quickly," said Ali quietly, as Susie froze in fright half way towards the door. "Just get out *now*, Susie!" Ali pushed Susie out, and turned to Lynsey.

But the rage subsided as quickly as it came, and Lynsey started crumbling even as Ali looked at her. Her eyes filled with tears, her skin turned deathly pale.

"I miss Kate a lot—" she wailed. . . .

A short time later Ali went to look for Susie, feeling a little concerned for her. Susie was in the attic, which was a kind of secret place that the sixth-form girls had found when researching the school's history. It was marked out of bounds, but no one ever came to check who might be there.

The place was full of memories of Summervale's long past: boxes of ancient files, costumes from old school plays. Along one crumbling wall stood piles of mildewed books. There were heaps of broken chairs.

The air was musty, and cobwebs lined the walls. A single low-powered light failed to dispel the gloom. Shadows hung down like ghouls and hid in murky pools. Struts and beams creaked with wear.

Susie was sitting on an old chest that was packed to the brim with books. Her brown hair framed her face, her eyes looked full of woe. She seemed so alone that Ali's heart went out, and she touched her on the arm.

"Are you okay?" she asked, as she crouched in front of her.

Susie gave a little nod. "Yes, I'm okay," she said. "I don't know why it is that she always picks on me. I haven't done anything."

"You know what Lynsey's like," said Ali. "We all have problems with her – it's just the way she is. Lynsey's got this possessive streak, and doesn't like anyone hanging round near her things. She'll always blow her top – she always finds an excuse. But it's usually her things."

"I wasn't near her things," said Susie.

"No, but in Lynsey's mind just being there's enough. She's very upset about Kate, and needs to let off steam. She's easily upset."

"I get upset too, though – that's all I was saying to her." Susie peered in Ali's eyes, as if seeking to support. "It really wasn't me who put the barbed wire there," she whispered earnestly.

Ali believed her. It was instinctive. "I know you didn't," she said.

"Who do you think it was, then?"

"I don't know. An accident."

"Like the hair dryer in the bath, and Miss Sagan's strange fall. And Kate was calling out, yelling out *Mr Slade*! I heard her, Alison. My room's next door to the bathroom – I really heard her scream. I was the only one who heard."

"Then why didn't you tell the police?"

"I tried, but I was scared they'd laugh at me." Susie looked in anguish and her face was quivering. "What if I *didn't* hear, and it was just a dream? I thought it woke me up – but maybe in the dream the screaming woke me up."

Ali stared hard at her, unable to answer this, and felt the gloomy attic brooding all around. She sensed the germ of doubt which Kate once put in her, a germ which lurked there still.

Kate had said, "*He was going berserk, and it was frightening*—" What if Mr Slade had overheard? What if Kate said something to him, if only as a jest? What if she'd let it slip and he'd taken it to heart? What if he'd murdered her? Her thoughts clammed up at this for it seemed incredible. Not here in Summervale—

"I think you should say something."

"That's what I tried," said Susie. "I thought that if I spread it around somehow the police would hear."

And in fact this did succeed, and the girls were interviewed. But nothing new emerged.

# 15

Within such an emotional and highly charged environment as Summervale it was inevitable that the early rumours would hang around for a while. There were also new ones being added at a rate which made it hard to keep a check, and by the end of the night Ali felt almost ill from the spinning in her head.

She had to get away from it all and find some time for herself, and felt a desperate urge to go to see Danny again. Though she had seen him around the school on a few occasions, helping out Mr Potts in the endless gardens, she had not yet been able to talk to him. Two free periods the following afternoon gave her the chance to slip away and run off down the lane. It might not have been allowed, but she was far too tense to worry about that. . . .

It had started drizzling by the time she turned into the yard, and with no one in sight the school looked bare and grim. The owners were on a trip down south, trying to sell some stock. Danny had been left to run the place.

His blue estate car was in the cobbled yard, parked underneath a tree which sprinkled yellowed leaves. It had mud on its sides, splashed from the local lanes.

She started looking for him, loosening her anorak, hoping her uniform would not put Danny off. There had been no time to change, and during school hours they were supposed to keep it on. He wasn't in his green caravan, which was parked at the back of the riding school, nor in the main farmhouse where the owner's family lived. It took a while to track him down inside the last dark stall, where he was grooming a liveried mare.

Ali said, "Hi," as she caught him unawares, and felt her whole face grin as Danny turned to her. He made her feel good inside, and just to see his face was enough to make her day. He put the brush down and came to the half Dutch door, which was at just the right height for them to moon over. He had a grin in his eye, and in the dim half-light his looks were magical.

"How are you doing?" he asked, in his soft low-slung voice.

"I'm doing okay," she said. "All things considered."

"This hasn't been a good time for you."

"No. And then next week," she said, "they've got the funeral. There are a lot of rumours around."

"There always are," he sighed, "when things like this happen. It takes people unaware, and they don't know how to react. So what's the main one?"

"That it's Mr Slade," she said. "That he killed both of them."

"I can't see that," said Danny. "He doesn't look the type."

"Who looks the type?" she asked.

Danny just gave a shrug. "I don't know anything."

He pushed the door open to let her step inside, and as he pulled it back again they were standing very close. She looked into his eyes, as if seeking his soul—

"Did you kiss Kate?" she asked.

Danny seemed to think about it for a long time, as if he wasn't sure how he should answer that. But he shook his head at last and, with a half-sad look, he said "I never did."

"I wish you had," she said. "Now that she's not

alive. It would have meant something, you know? Something to Kate." Her body turned away, and she looked towards the horse. "She'll never be kissed now."

He stood behind her, and they didn't say anything as minutes seemed to pass while they remembered Kate. Remembered her laughing eyes, her hair all out of control – her falling off her horse.

But then Danny touched Ali and put his hands on her arms, and turned her in the gloom of the warm and musty stall. For a long time they just stared into each other's eyes. Then she threw her arms round him. Their kiss was ferocious, and almost made her faint. She dug her fingers in, and squeezed the back of his neck. Ali's blood powered through her veins as if her heart was on fire – yet tears were in her eyes. Ali was crying for Kate, just as she was crying for herself. Crying at the strength of love and the fire she felt inside. She could never let him go, and would kill or die for that. Danny must never leave. . . .

# 16

On the Saturday morning Ali went with Maxine and Lynsey into the local town. They waited for a bus outside the wrought-iron gates of the school, looking across the fields which stretched towards low, distant hills. It was an autumn day: summer had had its chance. Frost put a nip in the air.

They were all feeling subdued, knowing that Kate wasn't there. They thought how quiet it was, how still and cold the day. They stared towards a sun which looked as red as blood. A thin haze softened it. A cloud of rooks was wheeling above a stubble-field, peering down at the ground as if they'd lost something. They would never find it there, in all that stalk and chaff.

They flapped away again.

Maxine said, "Yesterday, I saw Susie Minter standing in the bathroom."

There was a long and puzzled pause from the two friends at her side. If this fact meant something it passed clear over their heads. Ali had to look around at last to say – "What's wrong with that?"

"It's the way she stood there. It was kind of ghoulish, as if she was imagining how Kate looked when she died. She didn't seem to care, and never got upset – but it should have meant something."

"I can't even look at it," said Lynsey, shuddering.

"That's what I mean – she just stood and looked at it." Maxine looked strangely lost as her eyes stared into space. "It should have meant something."

They saw the bus coming some way off down the lane; a tiny crimson blob which glinted like a flame.

"That Susie's just a creep who shouldn't be round here," Lynsey said quietly. . . .

The town was crowded when they got off the bus, and they had to wait a while just to get across the street. It was as if every neighbouring town had sent a party in to see what was happening.

Maxine wanted to split up, which wasn't usual, and Ali half-suspected that she was still upset. Not at the death of Kate, but with the jealousy that so often affected her. For in spite of her poise Maxine was very insecure, and Ali knew she'd been hurt when Ali grew close to Kate. Even now that Kate was gone Maxine was still aloof, and had not forgiven yet.

But they all had something, Ali thought as they strolled, checking the windows out, looking at coats and shoes. Lynsey had her paranoia, and the thick, possessive streak which led her to list her things. That was a really strange one – she was the only girl in school who had a list of everything she'd ever bought or owned. It could make her so intense that she would lie awake at night just checking through her things. Ali guessed that, like Maxine, it was insecurity – a way of handling the life at boarding school. Away from her own family with its strange, sibling jealousy.

Ali had problems, too. What were hers, though? She tried to think of them, tried to create a list of all the faults she had. But they weren't really faults, they were just *character*, and could one alter that?

Ali often felt alone, which gave her bad nightmares. She also lacked belief in her own abilities. Was that the same as them, an insecurity? Or was she really not too good? Because while others seemed to breeze through life, Alison despaired – and she could not decide if this was natural. She had suffered all her life from the fear that she was right, and those who built her up were wrong. It was only recently, since Danny fancied her, that Ali really thought that she might have some worth. And if he was taken away from her or turned his back on her, she wondered if she'd cope.

"Hey, are you with us?"

"Yes, sorry, Max," she said. "I must have been miles away."

"I'd never have guessed," said Maxine. "I said, about these shoes – do you think they'd match that coat?"

"Which coat?" said Alison.

A little later, though, the day turned sour on them, thanks to a group of local youths. There was a certain rivalry between the boys in town and the girls of Summervale who came in on the bus. It could range from jests and jeers, through fascinated lust, to ill-concealed hostility. On the whole the girls avoided it, unless they liked the boy – and they were not averse to flirting when they could. But while they were struggling still with the hole that Kate's death left, it was not a good time for this.

The boys were rowdy. They were sitting outside a pub. They all had tight jeans on and Doc Martens. They all had greased-back hair and somewhat greased-back skin. They were trainee idiots.

"Do you want to sit with us?" one cried, and half-rose to his feet.

The girls strolled quietly on; they'd been through this before.

"We've saved a place for you!" This must have been a joke, because they all split sides at that. "Hey come on, girlies – we ain't going to bite, you know—" The youth was *on* his feet and lumbering their way.

Another one piped up. "Hey, they're all from that school! The one they call the school for death!"

All three girls froze at that; it struck them to the core. Maxine in particular found it hard to go on. She spun round on her heels and stared straight at the youth.

"Hey look – she fancies me!"

The youth was grinning as Maxine took a step.

"What did you say?" she asked.

"I said, 'The School for Death'."

"Do you think that's a joke?"

"Ain't a joke for them," he said. "Them stiffs you're wheeling out."

The mood had altered, and the youths could sense it now. Tension was in the air, and their grins locked stupidly. "I said 'The School for Death'. Ain't that what you're doing up there? Your new curriculum?"

Maxine's look seared him. "Do you find that

funny?" she asked. "Do you think it's very smart to show stupidity?"

"Oh hey, she's lecturing me!" The youth laughed like a fool as Maxine shook with wrath. Her body was quivering with the tension locked inside, and she sensed tears of rage lurking behind her eyes. But standing in the street, with people looking on, she felt mute and impotent.

"Hey, what's the matter?" he said. "Cat run off with your tongue?"

"I wish *you'd* die," she said. "And die a horrible death." And just for a moment she thought to strike the youth. But Ali's hand touched her arm.

"Just leave it, Max," she said. "These boys aren't worth it."

"*No, we ain't worth it!*" they cried as the three girls walked away. "'*Cause we aren't good enough for classy girls like you!*"

The words rang in their ears for the rest of that afternoon. They did not get much shopping done. . . .

# 17

At just after seven that evening, in a pensive and somewhat muted mood, Ali left the west wing to cross the quadrangle towards the tutors' block. She had a pink scarf wrapped loosely around her neck, and a pile of heavy books locked underneath her arm. The north wind stung her ears as her heels clicked on the stones, and echoed in the grounds.

The school seemed gloomy and brooding. Oppressive walls reared up like tombstones in the night. Bare windows gave out light, but not enough to make the darkness turn away.

She was going to Mr Slade's room to swap some books with him, for despite her fears and doubts, at one thing she excelled. When it came to literature she was the whizz-kid of the school. Ali could waltz through it.

Mr Slade encouraged her and often lent her books, as if he'd set his heart on making her a star, and it was only recently that Ali's nagging doubts had interfered with the relationship they'd had. For it was common knowledge that Ali was his pet (a cause of deep envy amongst some of the girls), and of all his adoring fans (and there were hordes of them) it was her he liked the best.

*Not any more, though*, Ali thought gloomily; at least not from her side, with all her fears and doubts. Trust is a brittle thing, and it does not take too much to send it tumbling. Even in her own mind she could see the lunacy of blaming Mr Slade for Kate's untimely death. But trust has subtle ways, and losing one's best friend can change many things. . . .

The building rose out of a clump of ancient trees like a Gothic mansion. Most tutors lived in town or one of the surrounding villages, but three of the staff members were housed at Summervale. They lived in tiny rooms inside a crumbling hall, which was greatly underused.

Windows keen as hawks looked down on Ali's head as she crossed a lawn which wound through convoluted curves. The air was thick with the smells of damp soil and fallen leaves. The wind was cold as lead.

She pushed the main door open and stepped into a hall which must have rung with noise in former days. But now the only sound was caused by Ali's feet striking the floorboards. She hurried up the stairs, aware that she was late, though she could have taken her time because he had not arrived. But Mr Slade's study door stood wide open and a lamp was burning bright, so she went inside to wait.

It was warm inside the room, where a gentle gas fire hissed, and the lamp above his desk cast down a lazy glow. Soft shadows on the walls touched the prints and charts that Mr Slade had hung. There was a bookcase, which almost creaked with books. Some dusty souvenirs of places weird and strange. The main thing was the desk which took up most of the room, and could have served as a dead king's tomb. A pile of folders lay sprawled across the top. Two matching, ornate pens lay like a wart-hog's tusks. A long, thin paper-knife glinted wickedly like a goblin's sword.

She picked a folder up, but it was nothing good; just lists of conferences that teachers could attend. A mousetrap caught her eye, half-hidden by some books—

*There must be mice in here.*

And underneath the books, one corner sticking out, was a single folded sheet of pale blue vellum.

It was the kind of paper Kate had used when she sent letters home. Ali tugged idly at it.

It was a love letter, a poignant *billet doux*; written in Kate's best hand, with all her curls and swoops. It had come straight from Kate's heart and broached her confused thoughts. Ali's blood chilled at it. . . .

*My Dearest John,*

*It is almost midnight now, and I have been lying awake unable to find night's peace, for I am missing you, and all my thoughts are of you and all you mean to me.*

*It is more than ten hours now since I last saw you, and not the briefest instant has passed in that time when I did not see your face or murmur your sweet name. I am in love with you . . .*

*At last I have said it – I just came out with it. How many times have I rehearsed those heartfelt words? I am in love with you – I really love you, John. I AM IN LOVE WITH YOU.*

*I hurt inside so much, I am so in love with you, and it's so hard to speak with others all around. But in the hall today, when I stood close to you, I almost kissed your lips. I long to hold you, John, and ache to feel your touch. I yearn to give myself and feel no fear or doubt. I pine to kiss your face and feel your strong caress. I long to lie with you.*

*John – I love the touch of you, the very smell of you – when your hand brushed my hand I almost died inside. I felt that I'd been burned, run through with love's desire, and kissed the spot you. . . .*

Here the letter ended, right at the foot of the page, as though there may have been more, though it was missing now. Ali's stomach churned inside, and her blood ran hot and cold as she read through it again.

She could feel cold fingers running along her spine – could hear the voice of Kate coming out through the words. A desperate, yearning Kate, a fired, impassioned Kate – a Kate she'd never known. Like the affair with Danny, Ali knew nothing of this, had never suspected it, would never have dreamed of it – and yet was holding it, a sad and desperate plea to dark, forbidden love.

When was it written? Was this a recent thing, or something from the past that Kate sent ages ago? Did she meet John Slade, too, as she had met Danny? Why had he kept the note?

Ali's thoughts were swirling. Where did this leave things now, knowing a link existed between Mr Slade and Kate? Just as he had forged a link with the unfortunate Miss Sagan – his fated lover.

Had Mr Slade been at the riding school that Sunday morning? He often was down there, taking the younger girls. Could he have fixed the girth so that the piece of wire worked out as Max was walked along?

But the changing of the horses – he wouldn't know about that. Unless – the chilling thought came that it was meant for her. It was Ali's accident that Kate took by mistake. The fall was meant for her. And what if she had done the same as Kate had done? Had taken a late-night bath to ease her pain away. Would he have said to her, "*Why don't you take a bath?*" Would she have died like Kate?

What would he gain, though? What was the point of it? She ransacked her mind trying to find a clue. And then she heard his step on the floor outside. She shoved the letter back.

He came in smiling, full of apologies. He looked as though he'd run, his cheeks were slightly flushed. He walked around the desk and glanced down at his things. And then he looked at her.

She was almost panting as she felt him study her, wondering if he could tell from her face that she had read Kate's note. Was it set there as a trap? Would he see it had been moved?

"What did you think?" he asked.

"I, er—" Ali's mind blanked. What was she supposed to say? *Well yes, I read the letter and I think it's really sad. . . .* "I don't know what you mean."

He glanced down at her hands. "About the books," he said.

"Oh yes! They're really great," she said, as she dropped them on his desk. "I really loved them. Faulkner's particularly – a really stunning work, *The Sound and the Fury*."

Mr Slade nodded. "He won the Nobel Prize."

"In 1949. I know, I looked him up."

His dark eyes twinkled then. "You're way ahead of me. As you often are, it seems."

He raised the paper-knife and tapped it absently. "I've got another one. Where did I put it now?" He looked inside a drawer. "Oh yes, it's stuck in here with my old handkerchiefs."

He handed it over to her. "I think you'll like this one. Written by Sir Thomas Malory while in his prison cell."

Ali glanced down at it, and saw *Le Morte D'Arthur*.

*Le Morte* means death, she thought. . . .

# 18

Ali hurried back through the gloom of the empty quadrangle, glad to be in one piece. What did all of this mean, if it meant anything? There was no shred of proof, just her own tortured thoughts. The thought that here was a man in whom people placed their trust – and he'd killed two of them.

It didn't make any sense; it wasn't possible; the entire world believed that they were accidents. What made Ali so smart that she thought that they were wrong, and he was fooling them?

Her head was throbbing as she tried to reconcile her past affection for him with the way she was feeling now. She must have been so naïve to have had a crush on him without knowing his heart.

And did she really think that way, deep down inside her soul, or was it all a part of coming to terms with grief? Was she looking for a *real* explanation – that *It was an accident?*

She couldn't answer that, for the time being at least, although it seemed fairly clear that she should keep this to herself. Ali could not go around making a charge like that; it was not practical.

She went back to her room, the book hugged to her chest, and put it on the bed and sat and stared at it. Lynsey said, "Whatcha got?" and Ali shrugged and said, "It's just another book."

"From Mr Slade's room? He's always giving you books. What's wrong with the rest of us? We never get these books." Lynsey picked up a towel and stuffed it into a bag. "He never gives me any. Anyway, I'm going over to the gym now for a game of badminton. Do you want to come and watch?"

"I'd rather watch paint dry. What's Maxine doing now?"

"I think she's in the bath—"

Where death had struck just a week ago. . . .

# 19

But despite Ali's misgivings, and the doubts she was keeping well inside, the time of trauma appeared to have ended for the girls at Summervale. There were no more deaths in suspicious circumstances, no riding accidents, no more tragic love letters, and the investigations into the two untimely deaths were wrapped up by the police.

The steel of autumn skies faded inexorably into the leaden shawl of a British winter, and the term wound to its close in an unsteady attempt to regain normality.

That year winter came with a vengeance, and swept down from the hills with snowflakes big as leaves. It punched its frozen fists against stunned window-panes, and crystallised the trees.

The school was howling as wind raced through its halls, and Mr Clegg stepped up into another gear. As frozen pipes threatened to bring the school to its knees, he toiled to save the place. From dawn to midnight he ran from room to room, checking a loose valve here, a fractured gutter there. A wild wind whistled by as his accompaniment, and hunted him through his dreams.

Mrs Robbe, the unfortunate secretary, fractured her collarbone in a bad fall on the ice. But Mrs Locke stood firm, and the fiercest crack of the wind could not ruffle her hair.

And at last the girls went home to fires and Christmas trees, and the nightmares of the term seemed to have been left behind. But in the dead of night, if they felt all alone, dreams haunted some of them. . . .

Ali herself returned to north London, to spend the three-week break with the parents she missed so much. And late on Christmas Eve her mother found her crying, alone inside her room. She sat and held her, rocked her against her breast, ran a soft, warm caress through Ali's tousled hair. Her mother understood and bit back tears of her own. It was the time to cry.

Ali's father, outside the doorway, looked on

uncertainly, unsure of what to do. But he sensed the weight of it, and took his share of it, and together they chased pain away.

Then Ali looked up some of her old friends, and a group of four of them went to the cinema. They met a group of boys who shared their cans of Coke, and they let them walk them home. Inside the hallway, beneath the mistletoe, she kissed a skinny youth whose name was Tony Franks. But even in his arms it was to Danny's lips that she addressed her kiss.

She couldn't forget Danny and wrote to him constantly, and he sent letters back in his thin, flowing hand. He'd pigged his Christmas lunch, he'd been invited by the family in the farm to share their New Year's Eve. Most of all, though, Danny was missing her, and was counting off the days until Ali returned. She kept his letters wrapped in thin white crêpe paper, beneath her pillowcase. . . .

# 20

Maxine threw down her heavy suitcase, and it almost cracked the bed. "What a trip," she said. "Awful. It took an absolute eternity."

"You came by car?" said Ali, who was stretched out on her bed.

"That was a big mistake, I shan't do that again. Not in the winter." Maxine peeled off a silk scarf and tossed her flowing raven hair as if it needed air. "My stupid guardian aunts arranged this chauffeur chap who smelled like cabbages." She picked a towel up and dried the ends of her hair, her head cocked on one side, her features grimacing. "So how did you get on?"

"I came up on the train and then the minibus."

"I'm surprised they can still make it," said

Maxine, as she used a corner of the towel to dry inside her ear. "The roads are treacherous. All my poor chauffeur could say was, *'Flamin' bloomin' 'eck.'*" She said it in a deep, booming voice to imitate the man, then dropped the towel on the bed and shrugged out of her coat. It landed on the floor and she stepped over it to check her wardrobe.

"Still got those mothballs. They must be breeding them. Has Mrs Locke got shares in Lever Brothers Ltd?"

"I don't think Mrs Locke's got shares in anything, she's too refined for that."

"Don't you believe it." Maxine slammed the wardrobe door, and turned to examine the room somewhat reluctantly. It was like eyeing someone she wasn't sure about, but would have to live with. "I'll tell you one thing – I'll bet you ten to one that she's got her hair pinned up in all those little curls. Do you know she goes to Spain and she's got a man out there? She spends her holidays there."

"I don't believe it," said Ali from the bed.

"It's really true, I swear. His name is Don José."

"She hasn't got a man." Ali smirked scornfully.

"She's got a string of them."

Ali jumped up. "Now I know you're lying!" she said, and swung her pillow round to bash Max on the head. "She hasn't got a man because she's got *Mr* Locke – and she's in love with the school."

"The blessed Summervale!"

The two girls started laughing. It wasn't all that bad to be back at the school. Not when your friends were there and pleased to see you again, and had a lot to tell.

So they talked and they caught up, and Lynsey bundled in with all her bags and news – though most of that was concerned with the lonely days she'd spent with her weird family.

And all the time they were talking, the snow kept drifting down like it would never end. Until a thick white shroud lay over all the land, and smothered Summervale. . . .

The next day, as though death had never happened, lessons began again. Mrs Day had a head cold, and snuffled through her classes dissecting frozen frogs, and seemed to be under the impression that if she poked them often enough she'd find a cure in them.

"Frogs are very strange animals. The only animal killed solely for its legs—"

The girls all looked at her and then looked at each other. She could be strange sometimes. . . .

Mrs Locke had a *neck* cold, which seemed to be very odd – they couldn't understand that one. And poor old Mrs Robbe developed creaking sounds in her healing collarbone.

Everyone else seemed quite healthy, except for

Mr Slade who also had a cold, and sounded quite a lot like an asthmatic cow in his tutorials.

"Shakespeare's sonnets," he mumbled. "The major works of art which we'll be looking at. More than a hundred and fifty of them – but we'll be contenting ourselves with just a few for now." Then his voice soared majestically, or as majestically as his thick cold would allow, and he said (looking round as if to challenge them) – "Don't tell me this is bad."

He hitched his trousers up (he badly needed a belt) and scarcely glancing at the text began to pour out a sonnet. He did not watch the class but stared out at the snow, as if entranced by it. . . .

> *"No more be griev'd,"* (he read) *"at that which
>   thou hast done:*
> *Roses have thorns, and silver fountains mud;*
> *Clouds and eclipses stain both moon and sun,*
> *And loathsome canker lives in sweetest bud.*
> *All men make fault, and even I in this,*
> *Authorising thy trespass with compare,*
> *Myself corrupting, salving thy amiss. . . ."*

And so went on until his class was done.

# 21

A dream of falling: the dark ground rushing up, the night air screaming.

A dream of thunder and lightning: the thunder of the fall, the lightning of her brain as it went skewing out of her distorted bones to spill across the quad.

A dream of death in a very dark place; of silence in a tomb, a rose between her teeth—

A dream of death inside a lover's tender arms, his hands around her throat.

Ali woke up screaming and sweating; the bed-clothes in a heap, her nightdress round her neck. She thrashed out valiantly against the clinging hands of darkness without end.

It was a night of thick silence; earth smothered by the snow which was still descending; the fortress of Summervale a black and jagged hulk against a bloodless sky.

A dog was howling across the encrusted fields, its voice a lonely drone which wavered up and down. It was a heartfelt sound, which only emphasised the peace which lay around.

Ali shivered as she straightened out her sheet, and glanced across the room towards Kate's empty bed. Maxine stirred in the dark; Lynsey breathed one soft sigh.

The intense peace returned.

# 22

By the next morning the snowstorm had given all it had, and was moving off in search of other places to lay waste. The clouds were pulling apart like balls of cotton wool, the ever-thinning strands revealing slats of blue which almost nervously peeped out across the land, hoping to be welcomed back.

The sun was hiding, but was prepared to appear as soon as everyone had taken up their place. And the girls were going horse riding and, much to Lynsey's disgust, would have some company.

"That little cow's coming," she grumbled bitterly. "What is it with Susie Minter? Is she trying to take Kate's place? Wheedling her way in like we're too blind to see? She really irritates me."

She threw her boots down and watched them roll on the floor, her thin face clenched and drawn as if in agony.

"I really hate that girl. I wish she'd rot and die."

"Don't say that," Ali said.

Maxine agreed with her. "It isn't funny," she said. "It's probably just a temporary thing because she's all alone." Maxine was perched on the end of her bed, brushing mascara on with the aid of a hand mirror.

Lynsey kept scowling. "I still don't like it," she said.

"She'll probably give up, because she's no good." Maxine slid the brush away and dropped her whole face-kit into her cosmetic bag. She slid the zip across. "So try to show good grace."

"I'd rather hire someone to punch her in the face. I couldn't do it myself because I couldn't bear to touch the spotty little oik."

Lynsey picked her boots up and slowly pulled them on, trying not to let her mood ruin her entire day. But she didn't look too thrilled when Susie popped her head round the door to say, "I'm ready now."

Ali gave a friendly smile almost unconsciously, for all her thoughts right then were turned Danny's way; in the short time that she'd been back she hadn't had the chance to spend any time with him. She had only seen him briefly, when he'd once called at the school, and though she'd prayed he would look at her, he had not turned her way. And in the middle of a French lesson she couldn't leap to her feet to shout *"I'm over here!"*

So this was a big day for her, and one that made her tense with an accumulation of desire stretching back several weeks. She had a pain inside and her heart was going wild. This love was killing her.

She needn't have worried, though; as soon as she saw his face she knew that things were fine and he was still crazy about her. His eyes were locked on hers, and in the freezing air she could see his breathing still. The plumes of breath from his slightly parted lips seemed to just fade away as he stood looking at her. And at that point the sun burst through to frame him from behind with a startling silhouette.

Maxine said, "There's something odd about him that no one talks about."

"What?" Ali turned to look at her. "What are you talking about?" She felt a flush of fear run through her guilty heart; for no one knew about them, and if Mrs Locke ever heard she would forbid the affair.

Maxine shrugged. "I don't know. Some kind of murky past." She put on an accent; a lazy Hampshire brogue. She said, "*'The lad's okay considering all he's done—'*"

"Where did you hear that from?"

"I once heard Mr Potts telling Mr Bleak about him."

"That doesn't mean a murky past."

"It must mean something, though." Maxine changed her voice again, to mimic Mr Potts. "'*He aren't caused no trouble 'ere.*'"

Ali fell silent.

*What kind of murky past?* She did not know very much about Danny's previous life. She turned to stare at him just as he turned away to talk to two small boys.

Did Danny have the kind of past he was ashamed to talk about? And if there was something, would it be to do with her? Could something from a time before have the power to interfere with the way she was feeling now?

"Max isn't tacked-up—"

"He's under the weather," murmured Ali. "They left a message with the school that I might have to ride something else." But she didn't really want to ride – she wanted to be just left alone while she tried to work this out. . . .

Danny was disappointed that Ali was not joining them in an indoor riding lesson.

"I'm not in the mood," she said. "I've got a headache."

Danny looked duly concerned, and tried to touch her cheek. But she turned away from him, inside the dusky stall where Max was shivering.

"Do you feel okay?" he asked.

"Yes, I'm okay," she said. "I'll be all right in a while. I've got things on my mind."

"Well – I have to take the class—" He didn't really want to leave.

"I know. Go on," she said.

He watched her worriedly, then reluctantly turned away, crushing the thick, dry straw beneath his riding boots. When he was almost at the door she turned around and said, "Danny, do you love me?"

He turned to stare at her, steam drifting from his lips.

"If anything happened," she said, "would you protect me?"

"Protect you from what?" he asked.

"Protect me from anything."

"Of course. You know I would."

"I'm glad." She smiled at him. She did not doubt Danny, but felt the need to be sure, and looking in his eyes she could see his deep concern. It could have just been Maxine again, showing some jealousy, making her feel insecure.

"Go and take your class," she said.

He grinned at her as he slipped out of the stall, and pushed the half-door closed as she turned to smooth Max's neck. It was going to be all right. Danny would be all right. Max was going to be all right. . . .

But shortly after Danny left Ali, something else occurred to shake her confidence. She had gone to stand in the crispness of the snow-covered yard, a scarf wrapped round her neck, a hat pulled over her ears. She was staring out across the still and wintry land, to the hills like dinosaurs.

The sun was shining and the day was very clear. Hedgerows and walls were wrapped in snow like bandages. A pair of mopish swans was pounding through the air, seeking a place to land.

She could hear horses snorting inside the indoor school and Danny's patient voice telling Susie to sit back. She heard a crash of poles as Sultan once again dropped Maxine on a jump. It was life as usual for the girls of Summervale, except that Ali held a secret love inside, and she wondered how long it would be before her secret was out, and if she really cared. She could get into trouble – she knew what the school was like, how love and sex and boys were the constant taboos. The girls could go berserk, could crack up mentally, so long as they didn't have boys.

What was it with Summervale? Were they afraid of boys? Did they think the girls would give up on work to move into maternity wards? Ali was sixteen now, she was a young woman. She had passion and desire in her.

She heard someone coming, and looked round from the fence that she was leaning on, her arms resting on snow. She was surprised to see Mrs Locke crossing the icy yard, and looking terrified. Mrs Locke was so stately: it was very hard for her to slip and slide like that, and risk indignity. Ali's heart was in her mouth as she watched the Head advance, with almost regal unsteadiness.

Mrs Locke had a black cashmere coat on, a muffler round her neck, soft grey boots on her feet. Ali was amazed by her; she'd never seen the Head step outside Summervale. . . .

"Good morning, Alison."

"Good morning, Mrs Locke." Ali felt the urge to curtsey, as she so often did. Mrs Locke was so serene and inspired such reverence that it always seemed the thing to do.

"Are you having a riding lesson?"

"No, not today," said Ali – grateful for Mrs Locke's sake that she had finally reached the safety of the snow-capped fence. She had grasped it with one hand, which seemed to fortify her, and she straightened elegantly.

"My horse isn't feeling well. He's got a tummy bug."

"Oh dear."

"All the other girls are in the indoor school—" Ali turned around to point out the long, low building in which the lessons took place.

"It isn't serious?"

"Oh no, he gets it all the time. He's got

a twisted gut, and sometimes his food gets blocked—" *He's got a twisted gut?* Ali wondered if she should say something like that in front of Mrs Locke.

But Mrs Locke didn't seem to have heard her. She was staring thoughtfully across the quiet landscape. Even her clouding breath seemed fine and elegant, like a fairy's cigarette.

"It's a beautiful day," she said softly.

Alison agreed with her.

"Except for this wretched ice." Mrs Locke glanced round with some apprehension at the threatening journey back.

Then she seemed to drift away, and just stared around the school, as if she had a lot on her mind and had forgotten Ali.

"The young man who takes the girls – is he inside the school, giving a lesson now?"

Ali nodded. "His name is Danny," she said.

"Yes, Danny Morrisey," Mrs Locke said quietly. She seemed to mull on the name, then said, "I believe I'll take a look," and began to walk cautiously on.

Ali looked after her in some mystification. What was her interest in Danny – what was the significance of it? She never came down to the riding school, it wasn't quite her scene – too much mud and manure around. So why had she come there at this time? Why risk the ice and snow and the walk down from the school? Why not come down in the spring and bring her grey saloon? Why check Danny at all? And perhaps even more significant was the fact that Mrs Locke did not appear to have made the journey alone. For standing a little way off, in the thin slush of the lane, was the figure of Inspector Blair. . . .

"Hello, Alison." He hadn't forgotten her name from all those weeks ago.

Packed snow lined the sides of the narrow road-way where Ali had gone out to meet him, since he appeared to have no desire to actually enter the yard, and was content to stand idly perusing the place with a half-smile on his face. She was struck again by the easy manner he had, which neverthe-less appeared to conceal an inner seriousness. As if his smile was bluff, and underneath it all his mind ticked like a clock. . . .

"It's a lovely morning."

"Yes, isn't it?" she said. "What are you doing here?" She made it sound polite.

"Oh, I'm just passing by. It seemed a nice day for a stroll."

"Did you come with Mrs Locke?"

"Mrs Locke? No." The easy smile remained, yet she sensed something more, some humour at her words; as if Blair knew certain things that in her wildest dreams Ali would never know. "No, I'm just walking."

But why round here? she thought. Back round the school again, with Mrs Locke again. She thought things had been cleared up and the files had been put away: had they learned something new?

Her thoughts turned to Danny. Had they heard the rumours, too? Had they both wandered down to take a look at him? What could Danny have done that made so many people look for a fault in him?

"Have you been riding?"

"I'm not in the mood," she said.

And Ali was suddenly not in the mood for anything. Why did they have to come and mess the whole thing up just when she'd found someone. . . ?

# 23

The rest of that day was a dull and gloomy one as far as Ali was concerned. She left the chilly riding school a great deal sooner than she'd intended, for outside forces had taken over the place and spoiled its atmosphere. It was a place for her and Danny and their friends: Mrs Locke shouldn't be down there.

Nor should Mr Blair with his pleasant, half-formed smile; he should be somewhere else, pursuing crooks and thieves. He shouldn't be round there spying on Ali's friend; the man she thought she loved. What were they trying to prove? Were they trying to tie him in to something that the rest of the world seemed to have let slip by? Just because he had a past – what kind of basis was that for checking his every move? It was unjustified and completely uncalled for, and Ali worked herself up into quite a state. By the time the evening came she was wound up to explode.

And then the next death occurred. . . .

It was Susie Minter, who hurtled to her death from the lofty pedestal of a fourth-floor balcony. It was Susie Minter's form which flew down through the night to hit a paving stone. She landed in the quadrangle, between two rose bushes. Her glasses left her face and landed in the snow. In the chaos that ensued somebody trod on them.

But she didn't need them now.

And that was just the start of things, for even while the police were there throwing a cordon round with all their dogs and lights, there was another attack and someone in the school tried strangling Lynsey. Mrs Day discovered her slumped in a crumpled heap, a cord wrapped round her throat, thick bruising on her cheek. She'd been dumped like a doll at the foot of the main staircase which led up from the hall.

All at once pandemonium reigned, and the school was terrified; it felt itself under attack from some grim, deadly force. Through two swift chilling acts, dark fear and death came back, and haunted Summervale. . . .

# 24

All attempts at normality were quickly abandoned as Summervale reeled from the blow. This time there had been witnesses to Susie's deadly plight, people who had seen a desperate fight with someone on the balcony's ledge. Someone who flung Susie off and watched her lonely fall into oblivion.

There was also Lynsey, in the Summervale sick bay, being pressed by Inspector Blair to remember all she could. There was no doubt at all any more that the latest incidents were not mere accidents.

A killer was in the school and killing off the girls. Two of them were now dead and one had barely escaped. The world was cold and grim, and Ali kept thinking – *I am so far from home*.

She couldn't believe it; she was locked inside her room while uniformed police officers patrolled the corridors. The school was under siege while the terror stalked within. It could be one of them. . . . It could be anyone. It could be Mr Bleak. It could be Mrs Locke or one of the cleaning staff. The man who brought the milk – the girl who checked the mail and seemed strangely intent. What if it was a teacher? It *could* be Mr Slade – he'd had the chance to kill both Kate and Miss Sagan—

Yet Susie Minter, though, why would he murder her? Unless—

She didn't know. Ali couldn't think of a likely reason, but then she'd never known about Kate's love letter. Maybe there was another link between Susie and Mr Slade – maybe he really despised the girls. All of that smiling, his pleasant bonhomie – could it be just a front for an evil deep inside? Did he have something dark gnawing inside his soul, which was starting to emerge?

Ali needed to talk to Danny; she *really* needed to see Danny. She needed to hold him tight and feel his arms round her. She needed to use his strength to keep the dark at bay—

She needed someone she could trust.

# 25

"Danny Morrisey? No, he isn't here any more. He left quite suddenly."

"Oh." Ali was standing in the deep snow outside the door of the farmhouse, cold seeping through her boots, piercing her leg-warmers and pricking at her soul. Of all the gloomy things she did not want to hear, this one was quite the worst.

Danny had run off and left her without even troubling to say goodbye; right at the darkest hour, when she was most afraid, when she felt all alone. The school was going completely crazy, and everyone was scared, and he'd just walked away. How could he do that to her? Didn't she mean anything? Were all his words and looks just toying with her heart?

As she stared up at the farmer's face Ali felt thick tears emerge, and trickle down her cheeks.

"Are you all right?" he asked, his red face furrowing with consternation.

"Yes, I'm okay," she breathed, trying to smile at him, brushing the tears away. Ali had taken quite a risk by just simply being here, and to have it end like this was a traumatic blow; for, a day after the latest sudden death, Summervale was in what amounted to a state of protective quarantine. Ali had to clamber out through a hole in the east field fence, and sprint across the fields.

Her lungs had been burning and her heart was hammering by the time she reached the riding school, just as twilight fell. The place had looked cold and bleak and sealed up for the night. There was no sign of Danny's blue car.

And now Danny was not there, and a thick and bitter night was descending rapidly. And she had to retrace her steps along that creepy track, with its banks on either side.

It wasn't the best night that Ali could have chosen for walking that lonely path. The trees were creaking in the breeze which filled the air. Sudden, soft falls of snow plopped from the high branches. The power lines whined and hissed between the two bare lamps with their unhealthy glow.

This was a bad idea, she thought as she stumbled

on, her boots slipping like oil across the encrusted snow. Six times she'd lost her footing and only saved herself at the expense of a jarred right wrist. Where had he gone to? Why had he disappeared? When was he coming back, or would he never return? If Ali had had more time, and not been in such desperate straits, she might have tried to consider these things. She might have also had time to grieve for the luckless Susie, and feel a proper sense of shock at Lynsey's experience. She had seen Lynsey twice today, and the bruises around her neck were truly horrifying.

*It could be me next*, she kept repeating to herself; and the lonely track was not a good place for such thoughts. The lines from the morning hymn the day after Kate died kept running through her mind.

How did it start now? Something about "the encircling gloom". But then it hurried on to strike at the core of things. And over and over again Ali breathed out the words—

*"The night is dark, and I am far from home,*
  *Lead thou me on. . . ."*

The night was *so* dark it seemed impossible. The lights were fading out even as she looked at them. She realised that the snow had resumed and was now a smothering haze which made the lamp-light strain.

The trees were whispering, and the hedge was rustling. Something came through the night as if it hunted her. Ali dared not look back in case her fears were real, and the deadly threat was walking there. And it was *gaining* on her now, she suddenly realised. Whatever was close behind was moving closer still. Something was in the trees, something was on her heels. Something real was after her. . . .

She started running, pounding along the track, her thin boots sinking into snow that held her back like mud. She did not dare look back, she must not ever look back – for she would surely be dragged down.

Ali would be murdered in the empty, frozen night, with snowflakes for a veil and ice walls for her tomb. She would lie all alone in a cold, shallow grave. Foxes would eat her flesh. This should not be happening. She was too smart for this – too smart to walk alone in dark lanes after dark. Too smart to be alone with a murderer on the loose – oh God, how smart she was.

She began to scream as her feet crashed through the snow, and branches ripped her face as she slipped to the ground.

As she tried to pick herself up somebody's hands reached down – and Ali fainted.

# 26

Inspector Blair helped Ali get back on her feet, and brushed the snow off her.

"Are you all right?" he asked anxiously.

Ali nodded tensely. Her teeth were chattering, and she had to bite her lips to stop them trembling. She grabbed the sleeves of Blair's long, belted overcoat. "Someone was after me."

The Inspector nodded, and took a quick step back. He listened intently to the shrouding darkness. The only thing he heard was the barest rustling sound that the drifting snowflakes made.

"There's no one there now," he said softly.

"But there was someone coming after me."

"It might just be the wind. Night-time is very strange – we hear all kinds of things."

Ali gave a long sigh as she eased her tensed-up neck, and felt a twinge in her back where she'd bruised it in the fall. She brushed her thick coat down and stared back through the gloom. "I thought I heard someone."

Again the Inspector nodded, and offered Alison a half-distracted smile. "You shouldn't be in the lane at this time of the night. You should be in the school – that's why the police officers are there – to protect you."

"Yes, I know," she said.

"So what were you doing out?"

"I had to see someone."

"That's going to have to wait. You stay inside the school until we clear things up. You'll be much safer there."

Alison nodded. *As safe as Kate*, she thought. *As safe as Susie was, Lynsey and Miss Sagan*. In fact, the more she thought, the more Summervale school seemed the worst place of all.

# 27

That night Alison lay dreaming about the killer who was stalking through the school. Ali was the only one left now. He had slaughtered all the rest, and was coming after her. Through long-abandoned halls and tomb-like corridors a madman hunted her.

No one could help her, for the school had been cut off; no one could hear her screams for the howling of the wind. The only sound inside was the thunder of his heels as he strode after her. The sound came booming through the empty passage-ways – a chilling beat of death from some unholy drum which pealed inside her head and stunned her frightened thoughts until she reeled from it.

She saw no exit, and could not protect herself.

She could hear the swishing blade that he scythed through the air. She heard him slamming it into each wall he passed, gouging the plaster out. And she was driven upwards by every flight of stairs. Sent up towards a roof where long cloths flapped like ghouls. Pushed out until the wind was beating on her face, and sleet blew in her eyes. But he kept coming, crashing through every door; his long cloak billowing out, his fury like a storm. His shadow reached ahead to dim the faltering lights. Darkness walked at his back.

Her fear was awful: she screamed it to the night as she stared down on the quad where Susie Minter died. She saw the very stone where Susie Minter hit – and it was calling her. She could hear it clearly – as clearly as the wind which buffeted her face and dragged her to the edge. A wind which pulled her out and held her like a glove – a stinking leather thing.

She started struggling to get the glove off her face, for it had clamped down on her mouth so that she could not speak or scream. It was pressing across her throat so that Ali couldn't breathe – it was crushing the life from her.

And she wasn't dreaming – it was really on her face. As Ali opened her eyes she saw a black shape loom. It was bending over the bed and had its hand on her mouth—

"It's only me," said a voice.

She started struggling. *What kind of talk was that? Someone was killing her, and saying – "It's only me—"* She started kicking out, she tried to scratch his face—

"It's only me," he said.

It was Danny: Danny was holding her. He had a hand on her mouth so that she wouldn't scream with fright. He was trying to protect his face by holding down her arms.

Ali stopped struggling.

"What do you want?" she hissed as he took his hand away, then glanced across the room towards the sleeping Maxine. The other beds were bare: Kate had not been replaced and Lynsey was still in the sick bay.

"I need your help," he said.

"You must be raving mad. You shouldn't be in here, I'll end up being expelled." She felt real panic rise at the thought of being found out with a young man in her room.

"There are policemen all over the place. I'll never get out again."

Ali came over faint. "You seemed to get in okay."

"There are dogs out in the grounds, there are police officers in the halls—"

"I don't care – get out of here!" She tried to push him off as she struggled up in bed, praying as hard as she could that Maxine wouldn't wake up.

"I really like you, Danny, I'm even in love with you – but you can't be in my room!"

She was desperate to get him out of there in case somebody came. Policemen were patrolling the hallways every half an hour. If one should hear them talk she would be packing her bags – she'd be drummed out in disgrace.

"They think I killed her."

"What?" Ali froze in the bed. She felt a blade of ice go tickling down her spine.

He took a long, deep breath and whispered in the dark. "They think I'm the murderer. . . ."

# 28

**H**alf way up the stairs she almost choked with fright. *What if he is?* she thought. *What if he killed them? And he's walking right behind – And I've got my nightdress on, which is no protection at all. What if he really did? What if he slips a knife between my shoulder blades? Oh God, oh God. What am I doing here? How did I ever get into such a mess as this?*

He was walking right behind; she could feel him touching her dress—

*Oh help me, God*, she thought.

They were on the staircase which wound towards the roof, and stopped at the attic door which was her secret room. She had planned to take him there to find out what was going on – but that didn't seem such a great idea.

All of a sudden Alison felt very lonely. She felt exposed and frail and way out on a limb. She didn't want to doubt, but she still had the fear that he might murder her. Why should he do that, though? She tried to shake it off. She was just too up-tight; she was in love with him.

*But then Kate had been in love with him. . . . Oh God, oh God*, she thought. *What am I doing here. . . ?*

# 29

He pulled the door closed as Ali backed slowly away from him.

"You don't have to be afraid," he said softly.

"Don't I?" She didn't sound convinced. She kept on backing off into the attic's gloom, until she hit a beam. Overhead, a single light bulb was swinging lazily in a slight, persistent breeze. It made the shadows swoop like vultures coming down to feed around her feet. "You said they're looking for you."

"Yes, they're out looking for me."

"But I suppose that's only because they've nothing better to do?"

"No—" Danny gave a sigh. "They think they found a clue. But it was planted there."

Ali nodded, disbelief etched on her face, and clutched her shaking arms, feeling the goosebumps rise. "The police planted a clue. . . ?"

"No, not the police," he said. "Probably the murderer."

Ali backed away again as he stepped away from the door, and the look he offered her was one of deep despair.

"I'm not going to hurt you," he said. "I just needed to talk. I've nowhere else to go."

Danny looked abandoned as he slumped down by a wall, his fingers loosely linked in a bridge between his knees. The light shone on his face, showing the tension caused by his desperate state.

"They found my pocket knife where Lynsey was attacked. It was a kind of souvenir – it had my name on the blade." He pinched the bridge of his nose, as a sign of his troubled thoughts. "I lost it a few weeks ago."

Ali shivered. "And then they found it."

"But I didn't put it there, somebody else did." He stared down at his hands, shadows beneath his eyes. "I'm not a murderer."

Ali moved to one side slightly, still not entirely trusting him, but not sure of his guilt; afraid his deep brown eyes might hide a killer's heart which was toying with her own.

"You've been in trouble before, though," she said

softly, her eyes locked on his face as if seeking a clue. She hoped that Danny could come out with something good, to help convince her.

"I've been in trouble," he said. "But just for minor things. And I got put away for something I didn't do. When they caught the real villain they let me go again, but it's a bit too late by then. These things stay with you, and come to haunt you. You get one tiny blot and it spreads to a stain, and all that people see is this stain on your life, and not the man you are."

He picked a book up and began to toy with it, turning it absently between his strong dark hands. The room was whispering with the probings of the wind. Roof timbers sighed and cracked.

"I never hurt anyone. I never did anything bad."

Ali stared in his eyes. "Are you going to hurt me now?"

His life looked full of pain as he stared back at her. "Not if you begged me to."

"What are you going to do, then?" She was sitting close to him, her hands held in his hands, her hair touching his hair. The whispers of the night were like the sounds of mice scuttling around them.

He stroked her fingers. "I'll just hide out for a while."

"Why don't you go to the police?"

"What, with my chequered past? How long do you think I'd last? They'd just put me away and throw away the key."

Danny stood up and tried to see the night through a tiny window pane set in the sloping roof. But there was only snow lying before his eyes. A blinding layer of snow.

"They've got the lanes blocked so that I can't escape. It's like the world's sealed off, so that there's no place left. It seems just a matter of time, but even when you're trapped you still have some hope left."

"Where will you go?"

"I don't know. Up north. I'll try to find a place where I can start again."

"What about me, though?"

He turned to look at her. "I love you, Alison."

"I love you, too," she said, and scrambled to her feet and flung her arms round him and kissed him on the lips. And in that dusty loft she made a vow of love she thought she'd never break.

It was only later as she was creeping back downstairs that Ali began to think of all the things she'd learned: of Danny's tryst with Kate – he was there when Miss Sagan died – his disappointment when Ali did not ride. Maybe he blamed Susie because she *had* ridden, and taken Ali's place as if squeezing her out. Was one long kiss enough to overwhelm the fact that all these doubts were there? Ali's thoughts were in turmoil as she stood in a corridor, thick darkness at her back.

Then she took a long deep breath and found a police officer, and gave Danny away. . . .

# 30

But far from ending things, this act of Alison's took Summervale onto a dark new level.

The school had gone crazy when the news was first announced, though Ali herself felt cursed by what seemed her betrayal, and the sooner things calmed down and normal life resumed the happier she'd be. For she would never forget the fact that she had broken Danny's trust, even if it was the only way the truth would be revealed; and the cloud she'd helped remove still left a lingering doubt inside her own stunned heart.

What she needed was time to work things out, and sift her own way through her tangled, tortured thoughts. She did not need to be Summervale's new heroine, with all the attention that entailed.

She looked for solitude at the end of a busy day of talking to the police and calming down her friends. She needed time alone; though there was still one thing she felt she had to do. She had to see someone to try to put things straight, because she'd built a wall that she should never have built. She had to see Mr Slade to tell him things were all right, and they were friends again. . . .

It was exactly seven o'clock when she walked across the quad towards the shadowy tutors' block. The snow was thawing, and the paths were wet with slush. A new moon in the sky had ripped holes through the clouds. All the school's lights were on, and laughter filtered out. It was like Christmas Eve.

She had several books under her arm which she was about to return, thinking that Mr Slade would understand what that meant. She knew he'd been upset by the coldness she'd allowed to interfere of late. She wouldn't have to say anything, she would just have to give them to him. She'd say, *"Have you got any more?"* and he would start to grin. He'd reach behind his desk and say, *"Well – what about these?"* And she'd say, *"Yes, they're fine."*

That was all it needed – a bridge to fill the gap, then things would be complete and life would be back on course. And she'd say, *"What about this?*

*That Chaucer couldn't spell!*" And they would start to laugh.

His room was silent as she stood outside the door, but she could see his light was on. She stood there waiting, thinking he might be in the bath, because his private rooms were beyond the small study. He might even be outside, jogging around the grounds.

She pushed the door open. The gas fire was hissing, but that was the only sound. She called out "*Mr Slade?*", but he did not appear. The light shone on his desk, and on a pile of books which had spilled over it.

"It's Alison," she said as she stepped inside. "I brought your Forster back." He still did not reply.

"I'll leave them on your desk. . . ."

And then she saw his face. And all the blood on it. Mr Slade was sprawled on a pale-green carpet, one arm above his head, the other across his chest. He clutched the paper-knife which someone had brutally rammed into his ribs. He was conscious, but could not move or speak, and his eyes were watching her with a desperate poignancy. As Ali stepped back, stunned, and raised her hands to her face, he mouthed, "*Get help—*" at her.

# 31

Following on so quickly from the day's euphoria, the effect on Summervale of the latest incident was completely devastating. Police officers flooded the school and grounds again; local roads were sealed off, tracker dogs were brought in. The major stumbling block was that as yet no one knew who was responsible. For not long after Ali found him, Mr Slade lost consciousness, and was unlikely to recover until after surgery. Once again each shadow posed a dark, unknown threat, and friend mistrusted friend.

For Alison in particular this was a hideous time, as fear and shock combined with guilt at what she'd done. What she needed most of all was to have her friends around – but she couldn't find any of them. For Lynsey was absent from the sick bay, and Maxine appeared to have completely disappeared, and everyone else she saw was simply too afraid to spare any time for her.

In desperation she ran from room to room, seeking a friendly face, a kind and gentle word; but all she met were stares, some of which seemed to imply that she had cheated them. For the nightmare was continuing. They'd thought she'd made them safe, but now their fear was back. Their new-found heroine had only feet of clay, and had betrayed them all.

Alison was crying as she pounded up the stairs towards the attic room where she could be alone. Towards her secret place where no one interfered, and she could slam a door on the world. . . .

# 32

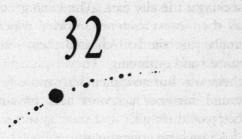

In the cathedral atmosphere of Summervale's vast attic the bang rolled on and on. The sound seemed final, as if the heavy door might be the lid of a tomb built to secure the night, and in its haunting gloom Ali sat down and cried as she reeled from the latest shock. She was in turmoil and her thoughts were spiralling into a dreadful place where fear and nightmares lurked; where love had been betrayed, and the one Ali had blamed had watched her helplessly.

The silence prickled, and the shadows gathered round. The echoes of her pulse seemed to pound in her ears. A cold wind kissed her neck as it climbed in through the roof. And she dreamed of murderers. . . .

Where did they come from and what kind of mask did they wear? Would she know who it was if the murderer came for her? Would she know how to act, what words to think and say?

She heard a stifled sound. It was in the corner; a murmur in the dark. The faintest burr of sound, as if an insect drowned. Within a heap of chests, sealed cupboards, old wardrobes – someone had stirred and groaned.

Ali was frozen; she couldn't move her limbs. She could not raise a cry or back towards the door. She could only sit and stare as someone kicked a door back on a wardrobe.

They were cloaked in darkness; they were lurching across the floor. They had their hands held out as if to grip her throat. They kicked through files and chests and stumbled over a chair, they were reaching out to get to her.

Alison screamed as the figure lumbered on, like some god-forsaken ghoul which had prowled the loft for years. Shadows burst from its limbs and crept across the floor – and Ali's shocked voice died. She couldn't find it, it had dried in her throat. Her arms flailed out like blades as she tried to fight death off. But the nightmare kept on coming, moving too fast to stop – then crashed down at her feet.

It was only Maxine, dressed up in blood and rope, as if she played a part in some dark pantomime.

Maxine with one long gash across her fine white brow. Maxine half-dead with fright.

And the door was banging in the gloom behind Ali.

Someone was walking in with evil in their heart.

Someone who slammed the door and turned the key in the lock.

Summervale's murderer. . . .

"I knew I hadn't tied those ropes tight enough."

Ali shivered as she started backing off, her eyes fixed on the knife which was aimed at her throat. She was trying to shield Maxine and drag her out of the way – but her friend wasn't helping much.

"Why don't you leave her? She's going to be dead soon. In fact you'll both be dead; the entire school is dead. I just set fire to it in the store-room down below. You'll smell the burning soon."

Ali looked around, trying to find some help: a handy length of wood or something for a shield. She saw a pile of books, but they weren't too much use—

"You'll never find anything. I know what you're looking for – something to beat me down. You think you can get away if you can get past me. You think you can break my arm, or make me drop the knife—"

Ali said, "Why, Lynsey?"

"Why did I kill them?" Lynsey gave an eerie smile. Her long white nightdress hissed as she paced across the floor. Her look was clear and blank, removed from all life's cares. She seemed strangely surreal.

"Why did I kill them? Because they kept on bothering him. I wanted Mr Slade and they got in the way. I would have had him too, if they hadn't interfered; but they kept on pestering."

The light shone softly on the knife Lynsey held out before her. Its long and wicked blade was like a dragon's tooth. She held it up to her face.

"I stole this from the kitchen," she murmured, as she kissed the blade with pallid, trembling lips. "In case I needed it. And now I really do. I'm very fond of it.

"He really loved me," she whispered. "But they kept pushing in and trying to tempt him away. And I saw a stupid note that Kate sent to him – and he was really mine. He really *was* mine—" Her face looked sad and lost, like a lonely little dog cast out into a storm. "He really was mine. He was the only thing I ever had to myself."

She turned away for a moment as someone in the school sounded the fire alarm. It seemed a distant thing, from some strange far-off land they were no part of.

"When I was growing up I was the last in line.

My sisters got it all. Do you know Louisa? They really worshipped her. They gave her everything that she could ever want. And all I wanted was love, but they kept pushing me off. '*Get out, Louisa's here—*'

"I could have killed her – I really wanted to. And then—" Lynsey's eyes dimmed with pain at the memories she brought back. "They said Catherine and Jane were so much smarter than me. They said I was really stupid."

"They didn't mean it, Lyn—"

"They said I was ignorant. They said of all the girls, I would be the one to let them down." She stared in Ali's face. "Why would they say that, Al? I was their daughter."

"I don't know, Lyn," Ali muttered desperately. "They must have made a mistake."

"They really hated me. And then when Mr Slade said I was *really* smart – well, then I had someone."

"But that's all it was, Lyn, it wasn't any more than that. He wasn't falling in love, he was just being Mr Slade—"

"Oh no, you're wrong," she said. "You're really wrong on that," and Lynsey's dark eyes flashed. She moved a little closer and leant towards Ali, the knife held out ahead as if poised to strike. "He really wanted me, but all those other fools kept getting in the way.

"Except for Susie," she said as she straightened up, and seemed to drift away as if into a dream. "Susie was just Susie, and I couldn't stand the girl. And so I murdered her."

The way she said it made Ali's blood freeze. There was no hint of guilt, no sorrow or remorse. There was nothing warm at all, just a chilling commentary on her campaign of death.

"I hit Miss Sagan, then drowned her in the lake. I threw the hair dryer into Kate's steaming bath. I tried the barbed wire to try to frighten her, but it needed more than that. And then with Susie, I lured her up to the room, and poked her in the face and pushed her over the edge—"

"But what about you, yourself? Somebody strangled you—"

"No, I did that myself. I stood at the bottom of the stairs and wrapped the cord around, and then just pulled on it until it made me faint. I fell the last few steps, which made it look for real—" She touched the bruise on her face. "I even planted Danny's knife to put the blame on him, in case they thought like you and suspected John himself."

"But you stabbed Mr Slade!" said Ali, glancing round as smoke writhed through the floor. She was trying to stall for time, yet it was obvious that time was running out and the school was well ablaze. The old, dried roof timbers were like a tinder box just waiting to ignite.

"Oh, but I *told* him," said Lynsey fervently, as if there was a point so obvious here that it was screaming out. She seemed frankly amazed that Ali could be so slow as to not appreciate it. "And he just laughed at me," she said, bemused by doubt. "When I said he was mine he just made fun of me. And when I said I'd killed those fools to stop them bothering him he went completely berserk. He was going to phone the police, Al – so I picked the letter knife up, and stuck it in his chest just to make him stop and think. But then he just fell down and – Ali, *I* don't know—" Lynsey looked full of despair. "It was so ridiculous." She turned to face the door, as if the school itself could understand her plight. "And now *you've* got to die so they won't think it's me, and will blame it on Maxine. I'll put the knife in you, and when the school burns down they'll find your bodies here and think she murdered you."

"But Mr Slade still knows."

"But Mr Slade is dead."

Ali gripped Maxine tight and said, "He's still alive. . . ."

## 33

"It doesn't make any difference. I have to murder
you because there's nothing else."

The smoke was thickening, and Ali was starting to choke. Madness filled Lynsey's eyes and
trickled down her chin. Ali could not recognise
the foaming, ranting beast which prowled in front
of her.

"I'm going to kill you for being so damn smart.
For having all the things that I've never had. You've
got your stupid home and I haven't got a home
'cause I'm a stranger in it. Nobody likes me,
nobody wanted me—" Lynsey paced back and
forth, waving the gleaming knife. "I should have
killed you all and had the place to myself—" She
stabbed the knife in the wall.

A length of plaster collapsed as she wrenched it out.

"We have to go, Lynsey, or we're all going to die!" Terror touched Ali's face as the ringing of fire bells ran wild in her shocked brain. "*We have to get out!*"

"We're going to stay right here."

"You crazy, stupid fool—" Ali climbed to her feet. "You're going to kill us all, and I don't want to die!" Panic made Ali mad. She grabbed a length of wood and swung it round her head as Lynsey gave a scream and lunged out with the knife. It glanced off Ali's side and tore a gaping wound as Ali howled and struck. The wood came scything down in a long, sweeping arc. It hit the swinging light and smashed it into shards. Gloom filled the smoke-filled loft as the plank continued on to slam into Lynsey's side. There was a sudden silence: a sense of pregnant shock. Ali could not see a thing in the darkness crowding round. She felt a tightening pain run down her shocked left side. Blood pounded through her ears. Her breath came panting as she took a wary step, the plank aimed out ahead like a blind man's home-made stick. It swung from side to side inside the lightless void in which she found herself.

She whispered "*Maxine?*" but there was no reply, though she could sense her near, as she could sense Lynsey. She may have been poised to strike, or lying on the ground nursing her injured side.

Ali put the wood down and reached back with her hand, groping across the floor to try to find Maxine. She saw the faintest light round the attic door, and decided to head for it. She would go and get help and bring some tutors back – they might control Lynsey, where she herself had failed. She took one cautious step, and Lynsey fell on her, like a monster born in hell.

There was a terrible screaming as Ali toppled back, Lynsey's hands on her throat, her teeth on Ali's face. Ali tried to beat her off, her feet straining to grip hold of something, her hands thrashing the air.

Dense heat was rising from the inferno down below. Thick clouds of swirling smoke were demons of the dark. The crazy, screeching bells formed an unholy wall of sound around the girls. . . .

"*Get off me, Lynsey!*" Ali reached deep inside, and found the kind of strength she didn't know she had. She wrestled Lynsey off and scrambled across the floor to reach the attic door. Her fingers stretched out and fumbled for the key. Lynsey gave one long shriek as she sped after her. The darkness bucked and roared as Ali swung her fist back and lashed out with it. She broke three knuckles as her fist met Lynsey's face, and Lynsey hurtled back and crashed into the gloom. Ali bit back tears of pain as she grappled with the key to get the lock open.

And someone was pounding on the door from the other side—

Someone was kicking it, creaking it in its frame—

As Ali scrambled back to go and find Maxine the attic door caved in. . . .

*"Lynsey's still in there!"* she screamed to Inspector Blair as he leapt into the room with two men at his back. But a sudden tongue of flame burst through the rotting floor and reached up to the roof. The room turned crimson as the flames came pouring through, devouring books and files and roaring like a beast. A solid wall of flame spread out across the floor and drove the policemen back.

*"Lynsey's still in there!"*

They were dragging Ali through the door.

*"She's going to burn alive!"*

They were pulling her down the stairs. Maxine lay in their arms, thunder was up above.

*"Lynsey is going to die. . . !"*

# Epilogue

They never found her although they sifted through the wreckage for two days. Maybe Lynsey got out and fled down a fire escape. Maybe she went to hell with all the crimson flames. Maybe she still lay there, concealed by ash and dust – Summervale never knew.

But at least the school wasn't burned down, although it had suffered a lot, and the upper floors were wrecked. The place would still survive without its murderer. Its life would still go on. So would Ali and Maxine. They would recover from their wounds and would survive their shock.

One day they would return, and once again walk the halls of the noble Summervale. . . .